THE GODDESS OF CRIME AND OTHER STORIES

STRANGE STORIES, VOL. 01

MICHAEL LA RONN

This series is dedicated to Ray Bradbury.
Live forever!

CONTENTS

AUTHOR'S NOTES

PREFACE

Welcome to Volume 1 of *Strange Stories*! I'm so glad you're here.

This series consists of short fiction I have published throughout my career.

At the time of this writing, I have written a lot of short stories. Some have been published in anthologies. Others have just been collecting digital dust on my hard drive, which is sad, so I created this series. Many of these stories are being published for the first time, though I wrote them long ago.

I've always had a complicated relationship with short stories. At the beginning of my career, they were the only thing I wrote. I was terrified of writing novels, so short stories were my safe place.

However, when I wrote my first novel, I got hooked, and I stopped writing short stories for a long time.

It's a lot easier to make money from novels; once you experience the magic of long-form writing, it tends to be the only thing you do unless you make a conscious effort to write something else.

But here's the wonderful thing about short stories: they don't require much time or investment for the writer or the reader. I can write a short story relatively quickly, build perfectly formed characters and worlds, and walk away. Readers can enjoy the story in one (or two) sittings. If I've done my job, you'll feel satisfied when you reach the end of each story.

There's also another practical reason I created this series. I took the Ray Bradbury Writing Challenge. Ray Bradbury was a prolific science fiction author. His work inspired me to pick up the pen.

Bradbury issued a challenge to young writers wanting to improve their craft:

1. read one short story, one poem, and one essay every night for one thousand nights.
2. write one short story per week for one year.

To say this challenge is devilish is an understatement. It's one of the most difficult challenges a writer can attempt because it requires mastering virtually every skill a writer must develop for a successful career: time management, organization, planning, writing, writing well, writing fast, business, marketing, and more. It took me several attempts before I finally "won" the challenge.

As I was reading short stories by other authors during this challenge, I often wanted to know what else they had written. This was especially true when I read speculative fiction magazines. To my dismay, when I encountered a wonderful story in a magazine, I found that many times it was the only piece of work that the author had published, or it was disconnected from what they were known for. For example, if an author wrote an excellent urban fantasy story but was known for science fiction and had no urban fantasy novels to offer, it created a disconnect. Usually, I stopped exploring that author's catalog and moved on to someone else.

I don't want readers to feel that way about me. If they read a story in a magazine they like, I want them to 1) know which titles in my portfolio the story is most like so they can buy them and 2) if there aren't any titles in my catalog in the genre of the story (because it will happen), I want to have a flagship product that will feel familiar—hence, a short story collection series where they can find similar stories.

I'll let you be the judge of whether I've been successful.

IN THIS VOLUME

The lead story, "The Goddess of Crime," is a magical urban fantasy featuring a lesser-known Greek goddess, but reimagined in a neo-noir world. "The Goddess of Justice" follows her sister. These stories came to me in an unsettling but revelatory dream. "The Goddess of Crime" appeared in the *Hidden Villains: Betrayed* anthology edited by Inkd Publishing. The anthology was funded in a smash hit Kickstarter campaign. ("The Goddess of Crime" also won Silver Honorable Mention in The Writers of the Future Contest, the highest award a story can earn before actually winning the contest.)

You'll also find two standalone stories from my bestselling dark fantasy series *The Last Dragon Lord* ("All Hallowed Roads" and "Return to Exodus Ranch"). If you love dragons, elves, and myths, you'll love these two. You don't need to have read *The Last Dragon Lord* trilogy to enjoy them.

Making an appearance is also a standalone story from my space opera *Galaxy Mavericks* universe ("Maybe Now the Stars Will Shine"), a story that first appeared in *The Expanding Universe* short story anthology series edited by Craig Martelle.

The story follows Devika Sharma, one of the main characters from the series on an important side mission that will determine the fate of the galaxy. Devika is a fan favorite in the series.

And that's just the start. From crazy uncles with magical powers to yachts sailing the world in an apocalypse to monster hunters looking for love after a devastating bodysnatcher war, this volume will keep you entertained.

IN THIS SERIES

Expect the unexpected. While I write mostly science fiction and fantasy, you'll find contemporary stories in these volumes too.

I write about heroes and heroines from all stripes of life. The connecting thread is that no matter what I write, it will be quirky—guaranteed. And of course, it will be strange.

As a bonus, each volume will have a special, exclusive extra "Encore" story. In the Encore story, I throw all the rules out the window and do something wacky inspired by all the stories in the collection. Think of the "Encore" story as an experimental lab where you can watch me play around with new concepts in real time. Maybe it will work, maybe it won't. Maybe it will be your favorite story.

(If you love the Encore story, do let me know when you review this book!)

The Encore story pays homage to "Annual" superhero comics that I used to read when I was a kid. At the end of a season, the comic writers would invite a new artist to spin a standalone story that often went into new and unexplored territory, yet was not connected with the previous season in any way. Annuals were notoriously zany. You either loved them or hated them. No in-betweens! Symbolically, that's where I like to live as an artist. I enjoy the high risk and high reward. It energizes me.

Give the Encore story a try. It will be suspiciously familiar, but with twists. All good fun.

Oh, and I always write author's notes for every story I finish. So, if you happen to read one of these stories somewhere else first, you can learn more about it in the Author's Notes section. This series will (usually) be the only place you can read the Author's Notes.

Thanks for reading, and let the *Strange Stories* begin!

—Michael La Ronn
September 6, 2024
Des Moines, Iowa

THE GODDESS OF CRIME

Here's what happens when you're about to get mugged.

It's nighttime, usually some blackened hour when you should be rolling over in your toasty bed. Your only excuse for being out so late is your vanity. You're one drink away from drunk, but you've still got your judgment.

The streets are deserted and rain-slicked. In the dark valley of buildings through which you walk, every window has its curtains drawn, like children covering their eyes while watching a horror movie.

A distant car horn blares as if trying to warn you. You see your reflection in an inky puddle under a flickering streetlight amid a background of pinwheels of light.

Above, the stars glitter like Turkish lamps, but they are not your compass home. Their beauty is a temporary distraction that pulls your eyes upward to marvel at the strangeness of the city that you've lived in for years but never stopped to admire.

You will be so busy staring at the breathtaking sky that you will not see the hooded man waiting for you in the doorwell two buildings down.

He saw you the moment you turned onto the street. You don't see him until you're a few feet away. When his hooded shape slinks out of the shadows, Mother Nature kicks in.

Your heart rate accelerates.

Your breath runs shallow.

Beads of sweat bloom in places you didn't know you could sweat.

That alcohol buzz burns away and you get as sober as if you never had a drink in your life. His shadow looms larger with every step.

If you run, he'll grab you. If you turn your back, he might hit you. He's got you right where he wants you.

If you have a knife, it doesn't matter. If you have pepper spray, it doesn't matter. It is too late. All those videos you watched on the internet about self-defense—just your imagination fooling you into thinking you could be your own hero.

If you were going to avert disaster, you would have done it seconds earlier.

The only thing that matters now—the only thing that's real—is your fear.

First, he'll ask you politely if you have the time. You'll look down and find yourself on the ground, tasting cement as he grabs your things.

Your watch. Your ring. Your phone. Your wallet.

You will feel light as his hoodie swallows your things. You will feel as if it has swallowed your soul. The urge to vomit will well up in your stomach, but somehow you will hold it down.

You will struggle, but he will be ready. You will hear the metallic click of a gun cocking and stare into the depths of its barrel as he continues his pillage. His gruff voice will tell you to stay down.

If you're lucky, he will strike you on the head as his getaway act.

If you're unlucky, he will shoot you, and you will die.

As for me, I will live. No harm will come to me tonight.

I invented the ancient art of mugging. It hasn't changed in five thousand years. The first man standing in a stone doorway in early civilization waiting by firelight to accost the first unlucky passerby—that was my design.

I hovered behind history's first mugger in an ethereal mist, whispering in his ear and telling him exactly what to say and where to strike. His every move was a prayer to me. When that innocent pedestrian in a toga stumbled by smelling of dry wine, I guided my subject's hand into the back of the fool's bare head. A few silver coins and drops of misery later, my offering was complete.

Any time a criminal inflicts misery upon the world, I grow richer and stronger. Yet, there have never been any shrines to my greatness. No one has ever painted a mural in honor of me that I know of. No one has ever uttered my name because history has never bothered to record it, and it is just as well. A goddess like me thrives best in the shadows.

As misery grew in the world, I didn't need the same foolishness as the rest of my brothers and sisters. I didn't need larger-than-life shrines on grassy hilltops to flatter my ego. I didn't even need blood. All this goddess needed to thrive was misery.

Now, the eons pass like a film on long exposure. Humanity has crawled away from its pagan origins, and most of the old gods are dead. No one prays to them anymore.

My dead brothers and sisters live on in paintings and myths that praise their lives. They live forever in the zeitgeist but will never breathe again.

Yet, I am here, but only because my subjects continue to

grace me with executions of my inventions: crimes of every kind.

I don't live on a hallowed mountain or in sun-drenched clouds. I live among humanity. I have a familiar but forgettable face. I blend easily in a crowd. You see me, then you forget me. Lovers throughout the ages have known me, and I have had to forget them.

Being a goddess in a world that has forgotten about your kind is a private existence. And lonely. You take your tributes where you can and keep living. No one you meet will last, and you cannot risk being found out, so you must always keep moving.

My travels brought me to this gray, sunless city covered with wet surfaces and shadows. I feel at home here because the unrest is palpable.

The crime is also exceptionally bad. I wear this city like an old warm blanket that I've forgotten but am oh-so-glad to have rediscovered.

While walking these streets among my faithful subjects, I sense her.

My sister is here.

It has been four thousand years since I've seen her. I sense her presence like a parched tree senses rain.

Walking through the shadowed streets drenched with fear and loathing, I use the stars as my map, my astral tea leaves. It has been ages since I've stared up at the night sky, but feeling her pulls me out of my usual drudge.

I stand in a darkened street and stare at the cosmos from whence I came, marvel at their everlasting radiance, and reorient myself in my sister's direction.

I must find her at all costs.

It just so happens that my path tonight has brought me into the path of our dear mugger.

This one's an amateur. I can tell by his hesitation in stepping out of the doorwell.

This isn't the first time I've been assaulted with my own method. Even my godly, forgettable face doesn't mean I don't get targeted every now and then.

Any other person would have frozen. Instead, I walk right to him, let him think that I'm playing his game.

I glance around. We're the only ones dancing tonight.

Then I meet his face, which I can't see but know all too well. The mark of innocence.

The teenager? Perhaps a child forced to become a man too soon. Dark hoodie. Stiff frame ratcheted back to seem taller than he really is. Except there's no menace. This noir street is doing all the menacing work for him.

"I don't have the time," I say, taking him off guard. He steps in front of me. I still cannot see his face.

"I don't give directions to strangers, if that's what you're asking. And if you think about following me, you will be following me for a long time before you regret it."

He studies me. Any mortal would be perplexed. "I've got somewhere to be, so if you're going to make a move, let's get this over with," I say, balling my fists.

One of the man's hands slides into his hoodie.

I smirk. "Okay, I'll let you strike first."

He draws a serrated blade. Military-grade. Curved with holes in the blade for a deeper, smoother cut. The kind that can disembowel someone without too much effort.

"Come on, honey," I say. I don't take my eye off the blade. I hold up my palms to let him know that he'll have an easy free-bie. "Strike fast and strike hard, my love."

Yes, most definitely an amateur. He hesitates, but not the

hesitation of a criminal before deciding whether to do a deed. His hesitation is about where to strike.

If you want to strike someone to kill, aim for their collarbone. With enough luck, you can hit the subclavian artery and send them to the underworld in minutes. Only amateurs go for the abdomen. It's a myth perpetuated by bad movies.

He goes for my stomach, but I sidestep.

I grab his wrist and shove it forward, hyper-extending his arm. The knife clinks to the ground.

I give this brave subject a sucker punch to the nose, then a sweep to an ankle. He's on the ground groaning and spitting out blood before he knows what hit him. I stand over him.

"This is the part when I'm supposed to be on the ground and you're supposed to be taking my things," I say.

He coughs into the street across from me, but I don't let him get away. Even an inch.

"If you were really good," I say, crouching and leaning in, "you would have killed me. But goodness—it seems that you are on the ground. Let's find out who you are."

I draw a little snub-nosed pistol I carry with me for protection and jam it into his forehead. With my other hand, I snap my fingers, sending ragged orbs of light that color the street tungsten as if someone flipped a light switch.

I roll back his hood.

A tangle of black locks falls to his shoulders.

Staring back at me is the bloodied and bruised face of a young girl.

Women worship me from time to time, but the vast majority of my subjects are men.

I stare at this girl in disbelief. I thought I knew this city, but it turns out there are still things that even a five-thousand-year-old goddess can learn.

"Who are you?" I ask. I press the gun even harder into her forehead. "Why did you attack me?"

The girl wipes a streak of blood from her cheek. "I have my reasons."

The fragility in her voice tells me she's not a threat. She can't be older than twenty-one. She's as thin as a stick, with rips in her jeans. In the moonlight, her face is a quilt of cuts and scrapes. Probably from street fights. This girl isn't winning any hand-to-hand fights, that's for sure.

"Your technique is terrible," I say. I holster my gun and extend a hand.

I sometimes forget that I can break a mortal's mind with my actions alone. She's got to be the most confused girl on the planet right now.

She doesn't take my hand. Instead, she doesn't take her eyes off me.

"You're right to be suspicious. You're probably thinking how crazy I am to be here talking to you and not running away."

I wiggle my hand again and soften my voice. "Don't worry, you're not in danger, unless you want to be."

The girl's eyes widen, then she reaches up. I pull her sweaty hand and she's standing next to me, smoothing out her hoodie. She takes a step back to keep her distance, then raises a hand to nurse her cheek.

"I could ask about your situation, but the story is always the same. Down on your luck...hard times...troubled childhood... You're only doing this because you have no choice, but you'd stop if you could...Sound familiar?"

She takes another step back, but I take a step forward, like a wolf stalking its prey. "I asked you a question, and I expect a response."

"You-you don't know me at all," she says.

I laugh in my condescending goddess way. "I know you better than you know yourself. You just don't know it yet. Don't back away from me. I'm not done with you yet."

I pause to see if my goddess charm is still working. It is. She can't look away.

I hold out my hand. The knife she used to attack me zips into the air and into my palm.

"Curious weapon choice," I say, holding the blade up to the starlight. "Not what I would've chosen. You should have used something more discreet. If you're going to go through all this trouble, why not just get a gun? Better protection, especially for you."

The girl's face hardens. "Why are you mocking me?"

I puff. "I don't mock. I speak truth. You're not exactly winning any street fights, are you?"

My words hit her hard. Her face contorts from vulnerable to the-wanting-to-prove-themselves look that young people are so good at putting on.

"No need to get defensive. You see, you remind me of a younger version of myself. I ran the streets too, you know. I've been the woman in the door. You know how that feels: lying in wait for some innocent sap to pass by. Surely you understand the fear running through your body the moment before you strike, don't you? Let me guess—you've only done this about a dozen times."

She shakes her head. "How do you—"

"Must you insist on asking questions I've already given you the answers to, girl?"

I hand her the blade hilt-first. "You must never hesitate. Even easy prey can surprise you. You must strike the same regardless of whether I am frail or a fierce soldier. You will never know who I truly am until you reveal yourself."

I point to the doorwell where she had waited to ambush me. "That was a bad choice. Even a drunkard could have spotted you standing there. Your only saving grace was that I was preoccupied with the stars. Next time, I suggest you inhabit a building slightly closer to the corner. That will give you the illusion of surprise. Then, you don't even have to ask them for the time. Strike and seize your spoils."

I'm breaking the girl's mind again. I hope she can take it. Her brain is one step short of a cognitive malfunction.

"I don't know who you are, but I'm done," she says.

I hold up a hand again. An invisible wall springs up behind her. She just doesn't know it yet.

"Sure, run away," I say. "But maybe I'm who you've been waiting for all along. Maybe I'm just what you need."

I grin as she turns, runs, and faceplants into the wall.

"Listening is another critical criminal skill," I say. "You would do well to try it."

I tilt my head at her as she rubs her other cheek. "Shall we continue your lesson?"

The girl glances over her shoulder. My senses sharpen.

Hurried footsteps are coming from half a block away.

"You've made a grave mistake," I say.

"Katrina!" someone cries.

A man.

Two men, actually, both wearing hoodies of course. They round around the corner, their blackened shapes running at me.

I shake my head and cluck my tongue. "Katrina, why didn't you tell me you were working with a team? That's a misrepresentation that's liable to get one killed."

I will her knife to slide out of her hand and back into mine. I laugh as the two goons launch their ambush.

The one on the left side of the street is lean, the kind who looks like he needs to rob people for money. If he had been the one who jumped out at me from the shadows, I wouldn't have thought twice about his appearance. I would've taken pity on him and given him something. He needs a sandwich—better yet, a three-course meal at a buffet.

The one on the right is the leader. More muscular, slightly overweight, and with a peach fuzz mustache. A proper deadbeat. He's the first to reach for his gun.

I like to play a game when I get accosted on nights like this. In the few seconds I have before these goons light me up in a blaze of glory, I predict that the first is a leech and the second is a lover.

I expand the invisible wall to encircle both me and the girl. Their bullets don't stand a chance.

The girl covers her head with her hands and crouches down. I detect a slight smirk, like she thinks this is the end for me.

I don't flinch as the bullets race toward me. My wall flashes red with each impact, holding the bullets in place for a few seconds before spitting the casings to the ground in a metallic rain.

I wait until these fools empty their guns. My ears ring like struck gongs. I yawn as I wait for the first trigger to click.

I flick my wrist as if shooing away a fly. Both men rise into the air and crunch into each other before collapsing into a pile on the asphalt.

"You have a poor choice of a boyfriend and your boyfriend has a poor choice of friends," I say. "Let me guess, Mr. Boyfriend is the one with the mustache."

The girl stares at her friends incredulously. I know I'm right—my instincts never fail me.

"Before this unfair ambush, I was giving your precious Katrina a lesson in true criminality," I say to the amateurs. "Would you like to join this private lesson, or shall I finish you?"

A twinkle draws my eyes upward. The constellation of stars on which I relied to point me toward my sister is fading. A few minutes ago, they had been bright as distant planets. Now, they glow like the embers of a dying campfire.

My sister is leaving the city. If I don't do something drastic, she will escape me. The thought of missing this precious reunion makes a knot catch in my throat.

I level my gaze at the woman. She keeps backing away from me and the two men lie groaning.

"The crime in this city is to die for," I say sharply, "but the education is lacking. I asked you three a question."

Silence.

"Answer me!" I shout. My voice echoes off the walls and slick surfaces and multiplies upon itself on its way to nowhere.

Mr. Boyfriend with the mustache rolls over. "Go... Screw... Yourself."

"Bad choice." I close my fist, imagining his heart in my palm. He screams and writhes like a wounded animal as I squeeze.

"Okay, okay," he says.

"Much better answer. Now stand up. You're going to make it look as if I'm having no mercy on you."

I will the invisible wall to disappear, though they can't see it. I glance up again at the stars. My time is running out.

"Before you three tried to ruin my evening, I was on my way to somewhere important. Because you interrupted, you will now be responsible for getting me there. In exchange, I will teach you about your craft so that your next plunder will be successful."

Mr. Boyfriend puffs. "Yeah, like you're a—"

I squeeze again, bringing him to his knees.

"I'm a what?"

Mr. Boyfriend waves me quiet.

"You're catching on. Which one of you knows the city the best?" I ask. Katrina's and Mr. Boyfriend's eyes drift toward Goon Face, who is coughing out a tooth. I note that he has an extremely punchable face.

"Very well. You. Have you ever stolen a car before?"

Goon Face jumps back as if I tried to punch him. "Hey, lady, I don't know who you think you are, but—"

"This city and its aversion to answering questions," I mutter. "Looks like you don't have the guts. That leaves Katrina or Mr. Boyfriend. Who wants the honor?"

The three look among themselves like terrified school-children upon receipt of the worst assignment ever.

I snap my fingers. "Katrina, you're up."

She shakes her head. "I've never stolen a car before. That's not exactly the safest thing to do."

"Now you're worried about safety," I say, walking away.

I don't look back. They will follow.

"Fortunately, I'm an expert at this. Follow my instructions and I will be with you every step of the way."

Stealing a car isn't hard. Technically, it's easier than robbing someone. The trick is to get the setup right.

My preferred carjacking method is the good old note under the windshield wiper. Preferably, it should look like a parking ticket. It should also be in a place where there is an irregular trickle of people, best if the parking lot is poorly lit.

The marks stumble to you like clueless animals. They wander through the dark, jangling their keys and laughing at a joke that one of them tells. Usually a couple. The passenger never sees the note; the driver sees it immediately and leaves the car door open as they inspect it. Then, my subjects strike. Forcing the passenger out of the car is just a formality.

I would love to use my favorite method tonight, but I don't have time. Tonight requires a more...brutal method.

I stand in the doorwell several blocks away from the place where Katrina assaulted me. The leader stands in an alley directly across from me, his back against the brick wall in a darkened alley. Goon Face hides behind a parked pickup truck a few yards to our left.

Katrina stands on the curb, ready to follow instructions.

I have no shame about what she is about to do, that is, if she follows instructions. The way I see it, by teaching what these three need to be more loyal subjects, I will grow stronger.

The headlamps of the car sweep across the street.

Across the alley, Mr. Boyfriend stiffens. He's ready.

Katrina shambles into the middle of the street, screaming and clutching an arm.

"Help!" she cries. "Somebody help!"

It's always a man who gets out. That sense of chivalry and the remnants of a bygone era always compel them to pump the brakes and get out to help a pretty young girl.

This man is no different. Why he's on the road at such a godforsaken hour and what he's doing in this godforsaken part of the city isn't my business, but his car is. Goon Face sneaks up behind him as he tries to comfort Katrina from her fake hysterics. He doesn't see the pistol crack into the back of his skull.

The four of us are in his car and driving away in seconds.

I sit in the back passenger seat. The car has comfortable leather seats and blood-red lights on the dashboard. A deep-voiced DJ plays late-night jazz. A lonely trumpet serenades us as a gentle rain begins to fall.

Goon Face drives. Mr. Boyfriend sits in the front seat, and Katrina sits in the back with me. I roll my window down and angle my head out of the car to see the stars. I close my eyes and let the drizzle wash over me.

I give Goon Face turn-by-turn directions.

I have no idea where we're going, but the stars do.

***

They ask who I am.

Because I want to play with them, I tell them an elaborate story. I tell them I worked as a special ops soldier in a distant country. They asked me what it was like, and I tell them they can never know.

"That where you learn to steal cars?" Mr. Boyfriend asks.

I take pleasure in the customs of this city by not answering his question. Instead, I glance wistfully at the endless fire escapes, dilapidated buildings, and helices of steam rising from subway vents.

Every street in this damn city is the same. Perhaps one day I will take up residence here. I could hide here for a long time and grow so powerful.

"That guy back there looked important," Goon Face says, wiping his nose. He drives the car like he is going to crash it. Stop lights are just a suggestion, and I get the sense that he has never used a turn signal in his life.

"If you want to do this for a long time and not get caught," I say, "do yourself a favor and obey traffic laws. It wouldn't hurt you to slow down."

"But you said you needed to be somewhere in a hurry," Goon Face says.

"In a hurry, not in a split second," I say. "You three truly are amateurs. Only amateurs drive like maniacs and wonder why they get pulled over."

Goon Face takes the insult personally. I let him have more. "But you've never stolen a car, just like you've never properly robbed someone, so what do you know? The techniques I showed you tonight—do them every time and you'll be just fine, as long as you obey traffic rules."

I check the stars again. We are getting closer.

I imagine my sister and what I will say to her. Where will we meet?

Perhaps she will be sitting in a graveyard when I steal upon her veiled figure and announce my presence. Or, she'll be entangled in a lover's arms in a late-night tryst. I've never wanted to see her so much in my immortal life.

"Where exactly are we going?" Katrina asks.

"You shouldn't ask questions," I say. "Besides, I'll make sure you get a nice payday when we arrive."

"That's definitely a bonus," she says.

Goon Face lets out a little laugh and shares a quick look with Mr. Boyfriend.

An alarm bell rings in my head. These three will betray me before the night is over. Even I'm not that stupid.

The rain mists the air as our destination reveals itself. Through shrouds of vapor and empty street after empty street, it rises up like a mountain in a dense jungle.

A hospital. I spot its neon sign from several blocks away. It's at least ten stories tall. A great fortress in the sea of drab. It reminds me of brutalist buildings I've seen in my travels. With bars over the windows, it reminds me more of an insane asylum than a hospital.

"You sure you want to go there?" Goon Face asks. "Who's at the hospital? Hubby?"

Katrina and Mr. Boyfriend laugh.

"I was thinking I would visit you after I finish what I started earlier," I say.

In the rearview mirror, Goon Face frowns.

"Pop quiz," I say. "What do you say when a patron hires you to drive her somewhere and then tells you that she'll pay you a bonus if you wait however long it takes?"

"Depends on how much she's paying," Katrina says.

"Very good," I say as Goon Face pulls into the portico, which looks like the mouth of an angry dragon. The word "Emergency" is burned out on the neon sign in the stone facia, and only the "Y" flickers like the light of a dying firefly.

"So," Katrina says. "How much?"

"Ten thousand if you don't complain."

I'm not going to pay them anything by the end of the night because they will betray me. That is also a lesson they must learn. There is a time and place for loyalty, but you better be damn sure who you cross. I look forward to teaching them this valuable lesson as I step out of the car.

"You two boys can wait for me in the parking lot," I say.

Katrina repeats my words and curses under her breath.

I curl my finger at her. "This lesson will be special."

She gets out of the car and follows me reluctantly, a puppy dog afraid of her shadow. But I desperately need her. The distance to my sister is not yet a straight line.

We stand gazing up at the uninviting building. Somewhere,

an ambulance wails. Above, the clouds drift in, covering the moon.

There are no more stars. I'm on my own now.

———

"Ma'am, we've got a backlog. It's going to be a long wait."

Katrina and I have walked into the hospital separately, two minutes apart. I stand, shaking my head at the green pastel walls and black and white checkered floor, leaning against a corner as I listen to Katrina argue with the late-night nurse.

The place smells like old plaster and sweat. A maddening hum from the overhead lights underscores the sad silence of this place. There are no windows here—probably by design as a reminder of your misery.

You're in for a godawful night if you end up here. In a hospital like this, you walk in hurt and leave worse than when you came in.

A dozen injured people sit in the waiting room like sad statues. A man with a gash on his head. A woman with an arm bent like a chicken wing. I wonder what brought them here. Probably my subjects. The misery in the room is like electric energy. I breathe it in and my resolve hardens.

I fold my arms and listen to Katrina.

"I need to be seen right away," Katrina says. "If I don't—"

"Four hour wait, ma'am," the nurse says

"I can't wait four hours!" Katrina cries. "I...I..."

Thud.

This girl learns quickly. I can't see her, but she's pretended to faint just like I told her to.

The nurse calls someone frantically. An automatic door swishes open. Another nurse. Both women hover over Katrina.

I use the opportunity to slip past and into the elevator bay behind the security desk. No one sees me slip through the golden doors into a stuffy elevator with a single fluorescent bulb. I'm on my way to the upper floors before Katrina even thinks about turning off her act.

I love subterfuge.

My sister and I share a special bond. She's the only goddess I respect. The only one I call my equal, and my opposite.

Our mother loved us, but she never showed me the same affection she showed my sister. I blame it on the fact that my sister was more dutiful than I was.

My sister pleased the other gods, always likable, always laughing, and always ready to do any bidding asked of her. She was a natural ambassador of our kind.

No one ever came to me. No one ever regarded me or asked me what I thought about anything. Whenever I accomplished an impossible oddity, they would just sneer at me instead. What kind of goddess dwells in such darkness, they would ask. Even the gods of the underworld received more respect than me.

I hated them. I even grew to hate my mother, the goddess of night. The only place for a goddess like me was by herself.

I'll never forget the day I walked out of the pantheon forever. I surfed on a wave of shadow, rising tall over the gods. I told them that one day they wouldn't ignore me anymore. I cursed them all, even my mother. I wished them darkness and told them that one day that I would be more powerful than all of them.

I was just a girl then. I never thought I would regret my words, but I've lain awake at night wishing I could take them back.

All those gods I cursed...are dead. My wish came true, but at the cost of being alone forever.

I didn't curse my sister. I couldn't. I still loved her. She stood up for me when no one else would. I could always count on her to do what was right and just.

As the elevator hums to a stop, I sense her energy at full tilt. The elevator dings and the doors slide open. We are now on the same floor.

I'm in some kind of ward. It smells of antiseptic and disease. I look for signs, but they are all scratched out. I have no idea where I am or what kind of sick people rest here.

Then it dawns on me that my sister could be among the sick. Nausea overtakes me as I sleepwalk my way down this white hall sorely in need of renovation. The rooms are empty. Each bed is perfectly made, and the window in every room is open, curtains flowing in a gentle breeze. I taste the rain in the air.

My intuition leads me to the end of the hall to a closed door. I don't want to open it. I know she's in there, and I know I may not like what I see.

After four thousand years, I'm finally going to see her again. I'm finally going to reclaim a part of myself that I've lost.

Part of me wants to run away. Another part of me wants to destroy this place in a rage if what I think I'm about to see is true. I place my hand on the door handle. The iron handle is warm to the touch.

I take a deep breath and push the door open.

The sparse hospital room is a tidy square, no bigger than a bedroom. The window is closed, and the lights are off. A glowing rune of my sister's mark is burned into the wall—a golden scale with both weights balanced.

The first thing I hear is the gentle sound of the television. A late-night soap opera. The television speakers don't work very well and the characters speak in voices that remind me of stat-icky snow.

The only light is from the changing frames on the television.

Then, I see her.

She's lying on the bed. A labyrinth of wires and catheters connects her to an ancient apparatus that shows a stable and steady heart rate. She lies breathing slowly, her long dark hair pooled on the pillow under her. She is sleeping.

I survey the room. We are the only two here. There is a worn cloth chair sitting next to the bed as if it had been placed there for me. I take a seat and gaze upon my sister's sallow, sickly face.

How long has she been here? Who did this to her? This is not a state befitting of a goddess. Anger wells within me as I take her hand.

She opens her eyes. An easy smile drifts across her face. I tell her to conserve her energy, but my sister was never one to obey me.

"I knew you'd come," she says weakly. "I knew you'd come for me."

"What happened?" I ask.

"What did you think would happen in a place like this, my dear sister?"

I look away. "I'm sorry."

"Tell me about your travels and the wonders you've seen," she says. "You were always the more successful one."

I don't want to tell her anything. I just want to hold her.

"There is no place in this world for a goddess like me anymore. I have failed. What do you think life will be like in the next phase?"

"Don't talk like that."

"Will someone paint a mural of me?" she asks. "Will you make sure that I at least get that?"

"Just a painting?" I ask. "There are other ways to live forever."

"I think a painting would be...nice." A terrible coughing fit seizes her and I squeeze her hand, tell her to take her time.

Her voice goes hoarse. "It was your subjects, you know. They put me here."

I wince at the thought of my sister being accosted in a dark alley. This is my fault.

She takes my hand, and a tear jumps into her eye. "I've held out long enough. I can finally rest. But, sister—"

She holds out a hand and motions me closer. I lean in.

"You won't let your dear goddess of justice die without... justice, will you?"

A devilish smirk spreads across her lips as I recoil. My ears buzz as she laugh-coughs.

"In the name of all those you've harmed throughout history..." she says, rolling back her bedsheet. Her body is covered with dynamite.

I run for the door and scream as fire erupts around me.

***

The only way a goddess can die is to be forgotten by her subjects, but it doesn't mean injuries aren't inconvenient.

The explosion destroyed two floors of the hospital. No one died. My sister made sure there were no patients on the floors. Her blast was aimed at me and me only.

I spend a few minutes heaving in a stairwell, my body blackened and broken. I am just burnt skin and bone.

I tap into an ancient spell I learned from an old god.

Shadows swirl around my body and regenerate my skin. Every cell in my body still burns as if I'm on a grill.

I cry for my sister. She always knew how to make my life difficult when she wanted. She is gone now, forgotten to the ages.

Weakened, I climb down the stairwell and out of the lobby as firefighters rush in and begin evacuating the place. I wave them away as they ask if I'm okay. Of course I am.

I stagger like a zombie into the parking lot amid rain, mist, and swirling siren lights.

Katrina, Mr. Boyfriend, and Goon Face are inside the car, watching curiously.

"What the hell happened up there?" Katrina asks.

"Drive," I say.

"When do we get our money?" Goon Face asks.

"As soon as you drop me off," I say, directing him out of the parking lot.

We ride in silence for a while. I can't get my sister's broken body out of my mind.

Suddenly, Goon Face turns down an alley, against my directions.

I sigh. Here comes the betrayal.

"This is the part where you attack me for real and take my money," I say.

Katrina raises an eyebrow.

"I told you that I know you better than you know yourselves," I say. "As you ought to know, your betrayal means there is never going to be any money."

I reach up, grab Goon Face's head, and snap his neck. His foot lands on the accelerator and the car zooms ahead like a racecar.

We crash into a dumpster.

I punch Katrina and drag her out of the car, wrapping my arm around her neck.

Mr. Boyfriend tears out of the car, but I pull out my snub-nosed pistol and shoot him in the back. He crashes to the ground and stops moving.

"No!" Katrina cries.

She struggles against me, slipping out of her hoodie. She overpowers me in my weakened state.

Katrina is wearing a white shirt underneath her hoodie. She backs away from me, shaking her head.

A glow on her shoulder catches my eye.

A tattoo. No—a glowing rune.

Of a scale.

"How did you get that?" I ask.

Katrina grabs her shoulder and says, "She told me you'd be a bitch."

I aim my gun at her, inching my finger toward the trigger.

"Kill me if you want," Katrina says. "But she'll avenge me. I'll have my justice."

"That explains why you were such a bad criminal," I say. "You're a warrior of the light, then. Why didn't you just say so?"

"Thanks for the advice," Katrina says. "If you're going to do it, do it."

Now I'm the one hesitating.

I lower the gun.

Even Katrina is surprised. I can only watch as she turns and runs. She disappears around a corner, and I wonder if I'll ever see her again. For her sake, I hope not.

I cast my gun aside.

Above, the stars are shrouded by the clouds. The rain drenches me and the red taillights of the car cast me in a diagonal beam of red.

The only way a goddess can die is to be forgotten by her subjects, and it seems my sister is not so forgotten.

Her laughter reverberates through my skull, a mockery that she'll never let me forget. She'll be reminding me of this night a thousand years from now.

But at this moment, she's got a lot of explaining to do.

I stalk through the rain, back to the hospital to finish what we started.

THE GODDESS OF JUSTICE

One of the worst parts of the "goddess" job description is that you have to mingle with your subjects from time to time.

I've never made a public speech, but it's no different from standing on a stage in an auditorium full of people, all eyes watching your every move.

My hands go clammy. My heart accelerates to the point of a panic attack. I can...barely...breathe. When I breathe, it's shallow and ragged. My vision narrows. My stomach lurches as if I'm on a boat on choppy waters. I see mocking laughter on every face. I feel as if I am inside a tin can, with every voice doubling upon itself before it assaults my ears. I can't speak because my mouth is so dry. I just want to tilt my head back, scream, and will the world to dissolve around me as I heave.

I just want to be back in my glass atelier high above the city. All I want to do is to swing in my crescent moon rattan chair with my bare feet dangling over a seventy-story drop, stare out over the turreted spires of the city skyline, and into the permanent azure sky.

I just want to observe my subjects march like ants through the streets that run like rulers on this circuit board of a city.

Give me a book. Give me ideas. Give me solitude.

But people? I am never in my element among them.

The problem is that I stand out in crowds. People want to talk to me. Like most goddesses, I have a familiar, pretty face, but I don't know how to communicate. The moment I speak, the illusion of me being a normal person shatters.

I stutter. I freeze. Look me in the eye and I will break contact and shy away like a wounded animal.

My brothers and sisters always found my lack of social skills amusing. My mother always said that I never had "goddess presence." When a god walks into a room, you know they're there. When I walk into a room, I'm just a geeky, nervous mess. I find the nearest corner and stay there. The only difference between me and your typical geeky girl is that I can destroy you.

There is only one thing that can pull me from my glass alcove in the sky. One thing that will drag me muttering through the sterile, carpeted bowels of the gunmetal skyscraper where I live, through the revolving glass doors, and into the sunshine-laced streets of this perfect city. A chance meeting that makes braving humanity worth it.

I invented the ancient art of justice five thousand years ago.

One starry night, a drunken fool staggered home and failed to see humanity's first criminal standing in a shadowed doorway, waiting for him.

One blow to the head, a stolen coin pouch later, and a few minutes of lying in a pool of his own blood, I appeared to him in a sparkling mist like a vision from a dream. He reached out to touch me, and I became his muse.

I stanched his bleeding, stitched closed his wounds, and smoothed them out until they were dry and rugged. I guided him to the city's officials. I was with him when he led a group of soldiers through the city, knocking on every door with swords drawn.

I whispered in his ear as he spilled the entrails of that criminal on the sand. I led him to the location of every spent coin. Justice was born that day.

To suffer injustice is an invitation to dance with me. I stalk injustice as a cat stalks a wounded mouse. Every act of justice in this world is the equivalent of prayer that makes me grow strong.

When I first stumbled upon this city with its permanent sunlight, I wasn't sure about it. There were too many subjects, too many people to encounter. I preferred towns where I could hide more easily. A goddess like me thrives in privacy.

But my subjects kept honoring me. Everywhere I turned was a prayer. Two people getting along on a street corner. An orderly system of resolving conflicts. No crime, no blood, no guile that cities are famous for. Just a peaceful place trying its best. So I built a home here, far above my subjects, where I could receive their offerings and keep a watchful eye.

Though this city is bathed in perpetual sunshine, I can see some stars in the gradients of blue and white. Their bone-white fragments sparkle today brighter than they've ever sparkled before.

That tell-tale familiar triangle in the southeastern quadrant draws me down to the street like a sleepwalking child.

I sense her. My sister is in the city.

Now, here I stand, among the people.

And, of course, it's just my luck that a giant bus is barreling straight for me.

The bus jumps the curb. Through the window, the overweight bus driver in his neon pink uniform has the steering wheel in an iron grip. He is screaming.

Behind him, a hundred faces gasp. Grimace. Close their eyes.

The bus's brakes screech like mad rats. The only thing standing between it and a building full of retail shops and flabbergasted people...is me.

My heart freezes. I dig my heels into the asphalt and arch forward, thrusting up my palms.

I close my eyes.

Silence sweeps across the street.

I open one eye, wincing. Smoke slants through the air, dissipating into a giant chrome grill. The bus engine's warmth radiates inches from my face like a furnace.

I open my other eye. "Oh no," I say. "Oh no, oh no, oh no."

I turn to run away, back into the revolving door of my building and into safety.

But a crowd has gathered in a circle around me at least three people deep. They stare at me with their jaws agape.

I turn three hundred and sixty degrees, looking for a way out. There isn't one.

I curse under my breath as the crowd erupts into applause. All these people—they're smiling at me. Cheering!

The door on the bus opens with a pneumatic hiss. The bus driver, in his neon pink polo and hat that reminds me of a denim folded swan, runs out and embraces me.

I pull back from him, nearly choking on his thick, musky cologne.

"I don't know who you are or what the hell you just did, but you are our hero," he says. "The brakes just stopped working—no idea why."

My heart accelerates into a jungle rhythm and I can't breathe. The murmuring voices around me blend into a bitter soup.

I fall to my knees. I can't speak.

"I... I..."

I become a robot with a chip malfunction. I want to say that I am not a hero, but the words stall on my lips.

"You okay?" the bus driver asks.

I want to run away, but the bus driver grabs me by the arm and says, "The authorities are on the way. We'll get you some help."

My head. Suddenly, I can't see. Whiteness flows across my vision like agitated milk.

The people. They have surrounded me with cameras. Every lens flashes.

Somewhere very, very close, a woman laughs. It's a full-throated, head-tilted-back kind of cackle, the kind my sister excels at.

It's her. The laugh grows quieter as she walks away.

Sirens wail nearby, and everyone surrounds me as I faint.

Naturally, the authorities detain me for questioning. It's what any rational police department would do when a random woman stops a bus with psychokinetic energy.

I awaken to the sharp smell of ammonia. I scrunch up my nose and want to vomit.

A circular white ceiling light settles into focus. A fly is perched upside down on it. It stares at me before it buzzes away.

Two faceless men speak kindly to me and help me off a wooden cot. They each take an arm and guide me through a white hallway with smooth floors and oval glass panels on both sides. One of the oval panels slides open and they sit me down at a table.

An interrogation room. The glossy white walls with brown agate designs on them remind me of the temple of my birth. All I can do is fixate on one of the jagged spears of brown and curse my sister.

My sister always was the dramatic one. Only she would endanger a bus full of innocent people in hopes that I would hear the invitation and save them. Only she was capable of a cruel, sick joke like that. I see her wicked grin as she strolls down a dark alleyway, thinking of me.

The oval door to the interrogation room slides open and a woman in a white polo, neon blue vest, and dark pants enters. She has black cropped hair and an eyebrow stud. A silver badge is pinned to her vest with the city's seagull insignia with the nametag "Katrina" in gold. She can't be older than twenty-one. The officers in this city are young—when there's no crime, anyone can do the job.

"How are you doing?" Katrina asks softly. "We debated taking you to the hospital. Frankly, I'm glad we didn't have to. That would have made this conversation more difficult."

Her voice sounds like a little girl's. I wonder how she'd do in a real city full of crime. She makes eye contact with me, but I look away and tuck a strand of hair behind my ear.

"That was quite the spectacle back there," she says.

"I... I...wouldn't know."

Katrina's face hardens with suspicion. "But you knew how to stop that bus."

I am going to murder my sister now. I am sure of it. Unlike other gods, I can't disappear or transport myself across the world. I have to deal with my problems directly. My sister knows it too.

The only way out of this problem is to go through it.

"I don't know what happened," I say.

"Neither do we, which is why you're here."

I keep my face blank. She is using every interrogation tactic I invented. If I were a run-of-the-mill criminal, they would work.

"I don't know how you stopped that bus," Katrina says. "I watched the security cameras. I'm just as confused as the rest of my colleagues. But we owe you our thanks."

She smiles, but there's an emptiness behind it, another tactic I know all too well. There is another trick coming. A twist.

"Where do you live?" Katrina asks.

"I'm...just passing through."

"From where?"

I make up the name of a land that sounds distant and exotic.

"Does everyone have the stop-things-with-their-hands powers there?"

I sigh. "I told you that I don't know what happened. Can I go?"

The woman clasps her hands together and looks me directly in the eye. When I look away, she tells me to look at her. I do, trembling.

"This is normally a peaceful place," she says. "Everything runs on time. It's so safe here, you can leave your doors unlocked and walk the darkest alleys with no fear."

She leans forward. "But over the last few hours, things have been going wrong. First, we find a rune graffitied on the side of our police building. Second, a bus's brakes randomly fail, and you're there to stop it with your hands. Now, we've got an explosion at a power plant and a third of the city without power. And you tell me you're just passing through. Care to revise that statement?"

I want to curse. My eyes probably betray my anger, but I look down.

"I am not guilty."

The woman stands and puts her hands on her hips.

I glance up at her. "I am not guilty!"

She stares.

"I am innocent and you cannot hold me," I say.

"I know," the woman says, gesturing to the oval-shaped glass door, which opens. "You're free to go, ma'am. But we'll be keeping a close eye on you. Safe travels on your way out of the city. There's a welcome center a mile away from here that will be glad to arrange your transportation out of here."

I can't believe my ears. My subjects are...kicking me out of my own city.

This woman is doing exactly what she is supposed to be doing. Eliminating disturbances. But I am not a disturbance.

"I have a right to be here just like anyone else," I say.

The woman raises an eyebrow.

"I can lead you to the source of the problems," I say.

Here's what that officer should have done: she should have listened carefully as I told her about my sister without telling her about my sister—I left the goddess part out. She should have said, "Thank you for the information. Let's go and stop that crazy woman." She should have called for backup—a sleepy partner and a few other uniformed lackeys—and we should have stalked into the sunshine to find my dear old sister.

But Katrina didn't do any of that. Probably because I stammered and mumbled my way through the explanation, which, the more I thought about it, didn't make any sense at all, even though I told the truth. Instead, she nodded, told me that she would be back soon, and returned with two women in white uniforms. Before I could ask what was going on, they clapped electric handcuffs around my wrists.

Now I sit in a padded cell in the city's psychiatric ward, arms bound in a straitjacket, staring at the folds in the wall, wishing that I was a better communicator.

Oh, my damned sister would be rolling on a carpet dying with laughter if she could see me.

"I can't arrest you," Katrina said, "but I can detain you for a mental evaluation. I have a hunch that with you in a padded cell, the crimes will stop."

I keep playing her voice in my head over and over.

This isn't fair. This is *my* city. Justice is *my* instrument.

"I won't stand for this," I say, as if anyone can hear me. The padded walls swallow my voice. Even if I scream in here, no one will hear me.

"I won't *stand* for this!" I cry. The next thing I know, the walls disconnect from the ceiling and float like objects in a virtual reality experiment. The padding shears from the walls.

Somewhere, glass shatters. Someone screams. My straitjacket unravels, thread by thread, until it pools on the floor like spaghetti. I am hovering in the air now.

Then I realize that the screaming is me.

Farewell, psychiatric ward. I stand naked atop rubble and rebar as the wind whips my hair about. I wave a hand and walk down a hopscotch of debris, clothes materializing around my body in a quiet swirl.

There is a double-sided barbed-wire fence between me and the street. With a simple wave, the fence rustles into pieces, and I pass through.

The sirens are coming. That smarmy officer is probably thinking to herself, "Damn it, I was right." A knot catches in my throat at the realization.

I slip into a dark alley. Finally, a place where the lights of the street don't reach.

I lean against cold brick, listening as the sirens rush by. I taste the tang of fire and smoke in the air. I didn't want to blow the psych ward up, but they left me no choice. The best I could do was deliver all the employees out of the building in a bubble of safety that popped over a nearby park. I would never have been able to live with myself if anyone died.

But I committed a crime. I was a fugitive on the lam, running away from my subjects who were tracking me with the very techniques *I* had taught them.

I slide down to the ground, panting.

This is just what my sister wanted.

I had an idea.

In any city in which my sister slithered, dark alleys were her altars. Just as I was the patron goddess of police stations, courthouses, and city halls, my sister was the patron goddess of alleys and shadows.

I could talk to her here.

I wave a hand over a puddle. It ripples in response. I speak an invocation in my mother tongue. I whisper my sister's name three times.

This spell isn't perfect, but it works. My anxiety is on full tilt because part of the spell has gone wrong—only the bottom half of my sister's face appears in the puddle. The other half is obscured by a rainbow slick of motor oil. My sister smiles at me with perfect lips that curl into a sarcastic grin.

"Can't take a joke?"

"This is wrong and you know it," I say.

"This isn't a question of right and wrong. I thought you knew me better than that. Did you forget our encounter all those years ago, when *you* played a trick on *me?*"

"This city is mine."

My sister's lips contort from a cocky grin into a straight line. "So you think."

"Don't make me have to fight you openly."

"That would be a spectacle for your subjects to remember for all time. Have they caught onto you yet?"

She laughs so loud that anyone passing by might hear her. "By the way, this is a beautiful atelier you have here. Very tasteful. And this view is worth killing for..."

My atelier.

"Don't you dare touch anything!" I cry.

But my sister's face swirls away from the ink-dark puddle, leaving only reflections of a fire escape above me.

If my sister is at home, I need to return.

I know the city. I can be back home in just a few minutes. I start down the alley just as the siren lights wash over me.

"Put your hands up!" a female voice shouts.

Bright lights blind me. I can't see anything or anyone.

A voice on a megaphone warns that they will shoot to kill.

The police have me cornered on both sides of the alley.

Then I recognize the voice on the megaphone. It's Katrina.

"I knew you were the source after all," she says. "We can do this one of two ways, but either way, there will be peace in this city tonight."

"You... You didn't listen to me," I say.

Silence. Katrina is listening carefully now.

"I told you that I could help you," I say.

"And because we didn't listen, now you decide to hurt us?" Katrina asks. "That's brilliant. You should have left town when I told you. Unfortunately, you didn't get the hint."

Katrina's words send me into another rage.

"This is *my* city!" I say, rising into the air.

Muzzles flash. Bullets fire at me. I block them with a purple force field that springs up around me like a bubble. The gun flashes fade as I rise higher into the sky. Eventually, I see Katrina's and the others' faces staring up in awe.

"Will you listen to me or will I have to bring harm to this city?" I ask.

Katrina stares at me as if she's staring at the face of an angel. I imagine an operatic song around me as she questions everything she's ever known.

But if she is in awe, it doesn't last long. Her face settles into an angry frown, and she points at me, ordering her team to fire.

More bullets fly. My force field deflects them.

I have no choice but to fly away. I glance back at Katrina, who is barking orders at all the officers, demanding that they follow me.

I have lost my favorite city and the respect of my subjects.

I weep as I fly away.

Now they have brought out tanks and fighter jets to stop me. Totally unfair.

My powers deflect bullets and artillery. I just want to disappear and make these people forget that they ever saw me. I don't know how I will ever be able to show my face in this town again.

I fly low to the ground, my feet inches from the asphalt. I weave between cars as they honk at me.

A silver tank rolls directly toward me. With a push of my hands, I flip it on its side. The ground shakes as sparks erupt from the tank. The hatch flips open and a man crawls out, face bleeding. I feel guilty and hate myself because I didn't protect him better.

I cut to the left down a long boulevard flanked by tall skyscrapers that remind me of bubbles. Bystanders stare as I zip past in a purple blur.

A sonic boom cuts through the sky. A fighter jet.

My subjects want to make my life difficult. I can disable a tank without injuring anyone. A fighter jet? Harder.

I rise over the streetlights, past the middle stories of the skyscrapers, and into the open sky. The fighter jet zooms toward me.

I hold out my hands. The curved glass over the cockpit flips open and I jerk the pilot out of the plane. For a second, he is a neon-green blur blazing through the sky like a strange javelin. I give him a soft landing on a nearby roof.

I can only control one thing at a time, so the plane is in freefall now. The pedestrians below are screaming, pointing up at it as it dives toward the street.

Sometimes, I wish I had better powers as a goddess. Sometimes, I wish that I was more omnipotent. I fly down and land in the plane's cockpit. The entire plane rattles as if it is going to break apart. My bones rattle violently and I instantly hate this thing.

I've never flown a plane before, but I don't have to worry about the technical parts. The plane succumbs to my will, and I guide it upward and away from the buildings. Below, I can feel the collective relief from the pedestrians as I launch into the open blue sky.

The triangle of bone-white stars glitters brightly now. I nudge the plane toward the triangle, toward the silver needle on the skyline that is my home. With its 70-story height and asymmetrical yellow windows, it is a welcome sight after all I've been through.

Except there's one problem. A swath of blue sky over my atelier has darkened into a swirling interstellar galaxy of night and stars.

My sister is definitely in my home.

I see a line of fire as it erupts from my skyscraper, shooting directly for the plane. I eject myself from the cockpit just as the fire vaporizes the plane.

I fall.

***

Cameras watch me as I walk into the gold-trimmed lobby of my building.

The lobby is a marketplace of retail shops selling food, boutique clothing, and gifts. There is a bubble camera in every doorframe, and one in every ceiling corner.

These are my inventions too. I see every inch of this city. When cameras can spot every criminal activity in seconds, justice is just a formality. It keeps people honest.

I feel the glass eyes of the city officials on me the moment I enter.

A female voice calls my name. From its tinny, staticky timbre, I know it is coming from one of the cameras. Katrina.

"What gives you the right to destroy our city?" she asks.

"I'm trying to protect you," I say, pushing my way through the lobby. "Stay out of my way and this will be over soon."

"I have a job to do," Katrina says.

The words hit me.

All of this... Protecting the city—it was her job. If she failed, she would be cast out of this place, just like me. After all, my city has no place for people who can't uphold order. That was my design...

I want to grieve for those that I've harmed today. I've damaged them in more ways than they can even imagine.

"I'm sorry, Katrina," I say, pushing the button for the elevator.

"It doesn't have to be this way," Katrina says as the elevator rockets to the top floor.

"If only you knew."

As the elevator door opens, I shatter the camera with my mind, cutting off Katrina in mid-sentence. I step into my long, mirrored hallway scented with frankincense. I kick off my shoes.

I am home.

The oval-shaped double doors to my apartment are ajar. As I creep through them, my sister's trademarked sandalwood scent hangs thick in the air.

My apartment is a massive studio with glass walls on three sides. It has a chic urban feel. The slate floors keep the room cold. My furniture is sparse—only what I need. My only indulgence is a floor-to-ceiling bookshelf that takes up the entire western wall, with books crammed in it. I keep tomes of spells, novels, and other artifacts that I have collected throughout the eons that turn out to be useful to a goddess like me.

In the corner of the apartment where the glass bubble is the biggest, I have an egg-shaped swinging rattan chair. My sister's black, Medusa-like hair overflows from the top of the chair. She swings slowly. Her leather boots hang just off the floor.

"You ruined a really good thing," I say. My sister swings faster, laughing quietly.

"This was *my* city, damn it," I say, not giving her time to reply.

My sister hops down and saunters around the edge of the chair so I can see her sallow face. It hasn't changed one bit in the thousand years since I've seen her last. She smiles devilishly, her burgundy lipstick dark like wine and her brown eyes almost sparkling with amusement.

"You had a good run, sister."

Wrinkling her lips lovingly, she smiles and extends her arms as she walks toward me. We embrace, and she holds me for a long time.

I expand my rattan chair with a flick of my wrist so that it fits two. Together, we swing over the city in a slow, lazy rhythm.

"I know this was payback," I say, "but seriously, why did you have to endanger a bus full of a hundred people?"

My sister glances out over the city. She frowns, as if something heavy is on her mind, the heavy responsibility of being a goddess of a skill that I will never understand.

"You shouldn't expect any less of me," she says. "I didn't kill anyone. Aren't you proud of me?"

A fighter jet streams over the building. I almost forgot that the military was still pursuing.

"You did well," I say. "But this isn't fair."

My sister reaches over and gives me another hug and kiss on the cheek. "It never is. I didn't want to switch watch last time either."

"Yeah," I say.

I rise.

Two men in black shirts and pants enter the room, carrying a red divan. After them, several women in black dresses enter carrying large boxes that hum with orange energy—the energy of my sister's evil. They do not make eye contact. Their faces have the tell-tale look of glamour—they're at my sister's every command. They do not think for themselves.

"I'll take great care of this place," my sister says, chuckling. "I can't promise there won't be blood, though."

"And I can't promise that I won't be back without a vengeance," I say.

My sister holds up a hand and waves. "I wouldn't dream of having it any other way."

I take one last look around my apartment. I hang my head and all my things swirl together into a hulking mass of light that settles onto my back as a knapsack. I sag under its weight as I make my way down to the ground floor.

Night has completely engulfed the city by the time I arrive at the welcome center. The center is a 4x4 kiosk at the entrance to the city, manned by a short man with huge glasses sitting among racks and racks of maps.

"Where are you headed, miss?" he asks.

I tell him I don't know. He pulls down a map from the ceiling and hands it to me. "They say this place is nice this time of year. You just have to watch your back for the hooligans."

"Hooligans, you say?" I'm suddenly interested.

I study the colorful veins of a new, kidney-shaped city.

"Pockets of the city have terrible crime, miss."

"Maybe it needs cleaning up."

"That'd be wonderful, miss, but it's a tall order."

"My kind of place, then."

I pay him for the map and start walking.

I shouldn't have gotten sentimental about this city. I don't even bother to look back at the bubble skyscrapers or the orderly streets. When my sister is done, I won't recognize it.

A female voice stops me.

Katrina stands in the middle of the street with a knapsack slung over one shoulder. Two others are with her. Even though they're in plain clothes, I recognize them as those that I harmed. The tank driver. The fighter pilot. They watch me with wan faces that already know the pain of exile. My heart hurts.

"Maybe you can finally explain," she says.

"The city...it excised you," I say. Katrina doesn't even have to nod.

"Come with me," I stammer. "My children, you have much to learn, and there is a new city waiting for us."

I don't look back to see if they follow. I don't need to.

Seconds later, we are walking side-by-side out of the city, into a great expansive plain sparkling with fireflies. There is grass and rocks and hills as far as we can see.

We trace a narrow sliver of starlight through this strange new place as a gray cloud slips over the pale moon like a silencing finger.

HANGIN' WITH UNCLE FUNKY

When you're a twelve-year-old boy, you can only get beat up after school so many times before your mother resorts to drastic measures.

You reach the point where the next black eye might be permanent or the next punch to your face will send you to an early grave.

It's even worse when you're black and your only crime is not being black enough. Bullies like Butch Stokes had constant reasons to beat me up.

Butch and his gang of flunkies cornered me walking home after school and told me it was my time to die. The streets emptied like a western movie, and the only thing missing was tumbleweed.

Butch kept showing off his green leather jacket with a fur collar, strutting around me like a peacock as his flunkies laughed. He said I wasn't cool enough to have one. He said maybe I'd be able to get one in heaven and asked if I wanted help getting there.

I rued any day pudgy Butch stalked me, which was just

about every day now. This was supposed to be the last day of school. I was supposed to be celebrating the fact that I was not going to see Butch's mouth full of crooked teeth for three whole months or listen to his stupid creaky voice calling me a honky-wannabe or feel his mystery-meat-laced spit as he climbed on top of me and punched me and cursed me out.

It was 1974. I had a whole summer of books and arcade games ahead of me, and the only thing standing between me and that was Butch.

"We're gonna get your summer started right, Lenny," he said, slapping my books from under my arm. "Gonna start it with a funeral."

You'd think after so many fights that I'd finally be able to defend myself, but you'd be wrong.

With a frightened yelp, I disappeared under a suffocating mound of sweaty boys and punches. Every blow was like getting hit with a brick. My vision filled with Tweety Birds and stars.

I closed my eyes and waited for the Good Lord to take me.

Suddenly, the crushing mound lightened and I could breathe. I thought an angel had picked me up and was carrying me to the pearly gates that I'd heard so much about.

Instead, somebody tapped my cheek and said my name.

An angel?

No, my mom...

She was still in her waitress uniform at the diner she worked at, a hot pink dress with a ketchup-stained apron. Her black hair was in perfect curls on her head.

She had beaten off the boys with her purse. Butch Stokes was running like Fred Flintstone.

I wasn't going to die after all. But after getting beat up by my mom, Butch was definitely going to be planning my funeral now.

"Those boys are gonna kill you if you don't learn how to fight back," my mother said. She dabbed my bruised and bloodshot eye with a sandwich bag full of ice. My left eye was almost swollen shut. "Leonard Jackson, I've had enough."

We were in the kitchen of the studio apartment my mother rented in the worst part of town. She was a waitress in a diner a few blocks away serving hamburgers, hot dogs, and other terrible cafeteria food. It was one of the only jobs she could get around here.

Somebody saw the fight coming and ran down to the diner to tell her about it. It was only three o'clock, but she wasn't supposed to be off until four.

"Why didn't you do like I told you?" she asked.

I was still shaking from the fight. I could hardly move or speak.

"I'm talking to you, boy," my mother said sternly.

"I... I...didn't get the chance, Mama," I said, tears streaming down my cheeks.

"You got to *take* your chance."

A tear jumped into her eye. She paced the rug in the kitchen, arms folded. "If you keep getting into fights like this, I'm going to lose my job. If you think I can step out of the diner to come take care of you every time some boy throws a punch at your face, you're dead wrong. One day, I won't be around to bail you out, Lenny, and you're going to have to stand on your own two feet and throw your own damn punches for a change."

She paused, the late afternoon sunshine lighting up her hair like an angel halo. She grabbed the phone off the hook and pulled the dial into seven half-revolutions. A man answered on the other end. She didn't have to say much before hanging up.

"This is going to be for your own good," Mama said. She

wagged a finger at me. "Your Uncle Funky is going to make a man out of you, and if he doesn't, then you can dig your grave, Leonard Jackson, because I don't know what else to do."

***

My uncle's given name was Cornelius Woodrow Wilson. Why my grandmama dedicated two-thirds of his name to the most racist president in American history is a fluke—she just thought the name sounded righteous.

So my Uncle Funky had a funky name. Nobody ever called him by his real name, and if they did, they got a wallop on the back of their head.

But that's not the only reason we called him Funky.

Uncle Funky was Mama's brother. He was the middle child of seven children, which probably explains everything, but that's just the starting point.

Uncle Funky was the kind of dude who did things his own way. My grandmama urged her children to get an education because the white man wasn't going to do nothing for them. Mama fell in with the wrong crowd, which was how she met my dad. My grandmama's advice was lost on her because she had to work two jobs to raise me. She didn't have time for an education.

I don't know what happened to my dad. Word on the street was that he was a heroin junkie.

Anyway, my Uncle Funky didn't go to school, which made my grandmama livid. He started a business that earned him a comfortable living. Nobody talked about his business for sure, but I always thought it had something to do with radios. Every time Uncle Funky came to grandmama's house for the holidays, he always had new radios for the kids. These weren't some rinky-dinky radios either—they were the real deal. The music was so clear and the voices sounded like they were in the same room.

Uncle Funky's business was going so well that the Vietnam War threatened to mess him up bad. And Uncle Funky had some funky luck too. The Man made him sign up for the draft.

Uncle Funky wasn't having none of that. He showed up at the Army recruitment center wearing a pink tutu and Cinderella slippers, with a duck on a leash. They say he went to a nearby pond and made friends with a mallard to pull it off. He even trained the duck to sit.

The government didn't want nothing to do with him. Dick Nixon would have had to be on the verge of nuclear war before he ever thought about recruiting Uncle Funky. And even then…

Top that off with my uncle's love of James Brown, and he got the name Uncle Funky.

He only came around on holidays, so every time I saw him, I was always fascinated by him.

Uncle Funky had a habit of just appearing out of nowhere. You'd be talking to him in the driveway while he was fixing grandmama's car, then go in the house to get something to eat, and he'd be standing next to you in the kitchen the moment you turned around.

"I learned how to materialize, man," he'd say.

When Mama told me I was going to stay with Uncle Funky for the summer, half of me was excited to spend time with the uncle who had more myths around him than ancient Greece. The other half cried because there would be a whole lot of books and arcade games waiting for me back home.

I had to leave all my friends, cousins, and my mama for three whole months. I didn't want to go. Besides, it was the last day of school anyway, so it wasn't like I was going to see Butch Stokes anytime soon.

Who was to say that Butchy wouldn't get hit by a bus or that he'd pick the wrong fight with the wrong kid and get his clock cleaned? I knew how to pray.

But Mama didn't buy it. "You're not going to talk your way out of this, Leonard."

And that was that.

When Mama dropped me off at the bus station, I couldn't hold back my tears. I hugged her like it was the last time I would ever see her.

The bus rumbled through sleepy God's country and endless highways that reminded me of snakes. On the final leg, I fell asleep with my head against the window.

Getting off the bus, I must've looked like an alien on a new planet. There I was in my threadbare corduroy jacket and jeans that Mama had bought at the thrift store.

The bus driver handed me my suitcase and I stood in the outdoor terminal among clouds of smoke and tired black people walking away with purpose.

I waited on the front steps of the terminal like Mama told me to. Nobody paid any attention to me.

It was a full moon, and the moon was playing peekaboo through thick clouds.

One by one, the passengers left, reunited with long-lost friends and family. The last car rolled out of the lot, and it was just me. A few terminal workers in gray uniforms swept the floor and joked around.

I started to think Uncle Funky forgot about me. I sat on the terminal steps with tears in my eyes.

Then, bright lights cut across the parking lot and a blue Oldsmobile Cutlass screeched across the asphalt like an angry eagle. The car stopped with a jerk, and the passenger side window rolled down.

A dark face with sideburns and a beard popped out. My Uncle Funky wore a tassel fringe suede vest over a lime-green flowery shirt.

"What are you crying for, Lenny?"

The inside of his car smelled like cigarette smoke and sweat. I sank into the leather seats.

"I got tied up with something," Uncle Funky said. "You weren't waiting too long, were you?"

I sniffled and wiped my nose. We drove for a little while in silence. He lit up a cigarette, took a long drag, and put soul music on the radio. "Love Don't Love Nobody" from The Spinners came on. Blaring horns and crooning men filled the car, and we rode with the windows down.

"Say, I hear some schoolyard bullies beat the stuffing out of you," he said. "That right?"

I nodded and told him yes.

"Man, that just won't do. That's why I told your mama to send you my way."

"Are you...going to teach me self-defense?" I asked. "I saw a karate dojo on the news. They teach people how to fight like Bruce Lee."

Uncle Funky let out a loud belly laugh. That laugh could make any party ten times more fun.

"Bruce Lee ain't got nothin' on me. But yeah, I'm gonna teach you a few things."

I didn't know where we were. Definitely the black part of town. There were big brick houses three stories tall, all lit up like Christmas trees. There were cars parked on both sides of the street, so many that Uncle Funky had a tough time parallel parking.

"Lesson number one, Lenny," he said. "There ain't no problem in this world that can't be fixed."

He pulled up to a spot between two Buicks. There was no way his car would fit.

"Think I can squeeze in there?" he asked.

"I don't think you can make that," I said. "Your car's got a big tail end."

Uncle Funky tapped me on the shoulder and winked.

"Just watch, Lenny."

Uncle Funky adjusted his side view mirror and backed into the space at full throttle. I braced for impact, but the car came to a smooth stop.

"Problem solved," Uncle Funky said. "Come on. I want to show you something."

We stepped out of the car. I didn't believe my eyes. When Uncle Funky picked me up, he was driving an Oldsmobile Cutlass. I'd seen that car a thousand times riding up and down the streets where Mama and I lived.

But now, staring at me was a Pontiac LeMans coupe. It had a much smaller tail end.

"How did you—"

"I don't know what you're talking about," Uncle Funky said, taking me by the shoulder. "Let's get you something to eat."

Uncle Funky took me to a house with a big red door and a lion doorknocker. He rapped three times at the door.

"Going to introduce you to a cool place," he said. "I think you'll dig it."

The deadbolt turned, and a black woman in a white dress opened the door. Uncle Funky kissed her on the cheek.

"You must be Lenny," the woman said. "Your uncle told us all about you."

She ushered us through the front door. I expected a nice home. Instead, we walked into a restaurant with fine white tablecloths. Looked like the kind of place you saw people eat at on TV. Adults were gathered around several tables, laughing and eating and drinking. Loud rock played on speakers in the ceiling. The place smelled like bacon, eggs, and coffee. Everyone was eating breakfast for dinner. There was another smell I couldn't place, like stale grass.

That wasn't the only strange thing.

I tilted my head. Sure, this was a restaurant, but something wasn't right. I was certain this house was a big rectangle. But the restaurant was a square, and double the size of what the house should've been.

I turned to Uncle Funky, but before I could say anything, he said, "Lenny, there are two types of people in this world. The first type only believes what their eyes can see. Like that schoolyard bully Butchy. Just a bunch of plain, reality-loving junkies."

He grinned. "Second type are the people who see things for what they are."

"Hey, Funky!" someone said.

Uncle Funky looked up at the ceiling and gave a big wave.

A man in an Afro walked upside-down on the ceiling as if he was right side up.

"What's that man doing on the ceiling?" I asked.

"Use your eyes, Lenny," Uncle Funky said, tapping his temple. "Maybe we're the ones on the ceiling."

My eyes adjusted to the dim lighting in the restaurant. Sure enough, there were tables on the ceiling too, and people were eating and drinking and laughing up there. A whole mess of people. They dined as if *we* were the crazy ones.

I fainted.

"Hey now, Lenny, that ain't no way to say hello."

Several blurry versions of Uncle Funky's face circled mine. I lay on a twin bed in a room with a slanted ceiling. There was a faded poster of Jimi Hendrix on the wall next to a vaudeville poster of Harry Houdini. That strange pungent scent hung in the air. It gave me a headache.

"That's the problem with you," Uncle Funky said. "You go fainting at every sign of danger. Is that what you do when they bully you at school?"

"Any person would have fainted if they saw a man standing on the ceiling," I said.

I sat up and caught my breath. The room was quiet and dark. Like a solemn triangle. I rubbed my eyes and tried to shake away the confusion.

"Uncle, do you do drugs?" I asked.

Uncle Funky let out that big belly laugh and slapped his knee. He must've laughed for a whole minute before he wiped tears from his eyes.

I had heard about drugs. I knew kids in my class whose parents were strung out on cocaine and heroin. I heard the drugs made you see and do crazy things. Everyone in my family also thought that Uncle Funky was crazy. This would have explained it. I told myself that this had to be the case. I *needed* it to be the case.

"I smoke the good herb every now and again, but you didn't smoke none," Uncle Funky said. "Even if I *was* doing drugs, which I'm not, that don't change what *you* can see, right?"

He had a point.

"You've just got to learn to trust your eyes, Lenny. What

you saw wasn't strange at all. In fact, it's stranger that you couldn't see it until I pointed it out to you. We're the normal ones, but we're not cornering the market on truth."

There he went with those funky words again.

Uncle Funky pulled the tab on a strawberry soda and handed it to me. It tasted good, but I still thought he was on drugs.

We walked down a metal spiral staircase back into the restaurant. My eyes grew accustomed to the place, and I didn't freak out this time that there were people on the ceiling—waitresses carrying food between tables and joshing with the patrons. A brown Labrador sitting under a lady's foot saw me and gave a lazy bark.

Uncle Funky and I sat down at a table. The waitress brought me the best ham and eggs I ever had in my life.

Uncle Funky lived in a tiny little pad over a pet shop. The wallpaper was worn and the place was several shades of brown. Uncle Funky made up a cot next to the couch for me to sleep on. If I listened carefully, I could've sworn I heard puppies whimpering from the shop below.

"Here's the deal," Uncle Funky said. "From now on, while you're running with me, you're going to be cool, got it? Nobody's going to mess with you. If they do, they're going to regret it."

"But, Uncle Funky, I'm just a kid," I said. "You're telling me that if I passed Andre the Giant on the street, that he would be afraid of me?"

"Why not?" he asked. "He might be beefy, but he's just a regular dude like you and me."

"All I know is that Butch Stokes is planning my funeral,

and if I strut back home thinking like that, he's gonna put me in a coffin."

Uncle Funky grinned at me. "I've been in a coffin before. It ain't no thing. All you gotta do is push off the lid and you're out. What's the harm in that?"

"Because I would be in *heaven*," I said.

Uncle Funky stroked his beard. "You got to pick a place, man. Either you're gonna be in a coffin or heaven. Can't be in two places at the same time. Which is it?"

I didn't know what to say.

"Put your things by the piano," Uncle Funky said, waving as he walked to the kitchen.

The flat had a lot of things. A piano wasn't one of them. Instead of complaining, I focused my eyesight on the apartment in front of me. All of a sudden, I wasn't in my uncle's tiny flat anymore. We were in a big royal mansion. The walls were covered with red-and-gold striped velvet wallpaper. A grand piano sat next to a window that overlooked a big fancy European city with staggered roofs.

"I was waiting for you to catch on," Uncle Funky said. "I always knew you were something special. You see, you and me aren't like other people. That's why those boys beat up on you. They're jealous of what you got. With a little bit of training, you'll be showing them the deal."

Uncle Funky pointed to my cot—now a big king bed with wooden posts.

I fell asleep the moment my head hit the pillow.

***

When I opened my eyes, sunlight streamed through the window. Uncle Funky had the window propped open and a gentle breeze blew through the room.

"Sleep good?" he asked, dancing in the kitchen with a skillet of grits crackling below him. "Today's the day."

After a breakfast of bacon and grits, I followed Uncle Funky downstairs to the pet shop. But the pet shop wasn't a pet shop anymore. It was a dojo.

A Japanese teacher in a white karate uniform with a black belt practiced some punches in slow motion. He clapped his hands together silently and bowed to us.

"Shall we begin training, Mr. Funky?" the teacher asked.

"This guy knows karate?" I asked.

"That and he knows ka-razy," Uncle Funky said. "Better look out, Lenny."

The next thing I knew, the teacher was running at me. He jumped into a flying kick.

"He can't hit you if you're not where he thinks you are," Uncle Funky said.

I turned away and yelled as the teacher zoomed toward me, yelling at the top of his lungs.

He never struck me. He hung in the air as if suspended by strings. Then he touched down and said, "We'll try that again."

"Remember what I told you," Uncle Funky said.

I had to be dreaming. This was like something out of a movie.

The teacher ran to the back of the room, tapped the mats on the wall, and ran at me again. He jumped into the air, aiming a kick at me.

This time, I stared at the sole of his foot, ready for it to hit me.

I didn't want him to hit me.

I wanted to be anywhere but here right now.

I just wanted to have a normal summer.

I should've been in the arcade or in an alcove in the library curled up with a book.

I didn't need this!

Suddenly, I wasn't standing next to Uncle Funky anymore. I was in the corner of the room. The teacher kicked where I had been, and he landed awkwardly on a knee.

"That's what I'm talking about!" Uncle Funky said. He clapped his hands and pumped a fist in the air. "That's the spirit. I told you that you were just like me. That's what I want you to do every time, got it?"

The teacher ran at me again and jumped into another kick. I tapped into the same thoughts and I materialized in another corner of the room.

"What is going on?" I asked.

"You're just realizing your full potential, that's all," Uncle Funky said. "Boy, your mama is not gonna recognize you when I'm done with you."

The teacher and I sparred more. No matter what kind of attack he threw, he never hit me.

***

"Why can't Mama do what I'm doing?" I asked as we sat at a lunch counter eating sandwiches. "Why can't Mama just change our circumstances and be rich? We wouldn't have to live in that tiny apartment. We could live in a mansion and eat like the Queen of England."

Uncle Funky took a big swig of coffee. "It's not that easy, Lenny. Your mama's a special woman. The rest of your uncles and aunts? I couldn't give a damn. Most folks don't want to see what life truly has for them. They walk through life asleep."

"But why?"

"Because if most people would open their eyes, they'd be terrified. They wouldn't be able to handle it. They'd go nuts, man."

Uncle Funky finished his sandwich and rolled up the wax paper on his plate. "But you—you're sensitive. You can handle it. I guarantee you that if Butch Stokes saw half the things you've seen so far, he'd be in the loony bin."

I hadn't thought about Butch in a while. Just the thought of going back to school made me lose my appetite.

"These powers belong to a select few," Uncle Funky said. "I want you to use them responsibly. Can you do that, Lenny?"

That summer, I hung with Uncle Funky. I was his shadow everywhere he went. I met all sorts of crazy people. We traveled everywhere in the world without leaving the city.

Most importantly, he taught me how to do things I never imagined. I learned how to materialize and how to do karate and how to turn a ham sandwich into caviar. When Uncle Funky took me to the bus station and gave me a big hug, I cried.

"No need to cry, Lenny," he said, handing me a bright red radio with golden speakers. "Anytime you want to talk, just turn the dial to station seven hundred. Remember what I told you about that bully Butch Stokes, now."

And just like that, the first day of school came, and the bell rang for dismissal. There I was, in my new corduroy coat, gray velour shirt, and backpack, walking home.

Two blocks later, Butch and his cronies slunk out of an alley, calling my name.

"If it ain't Lenny the wimp," Butch said. He smiled with a mouthful of crooked teeth and tossed his backpack on the ground. He threw a fist into an open palm three times.

"I sent somebody down to keep watch on your mama," Butch said, advancing slowly. "She ain't gonna save you this time."

I froze. It was as if everything I learned over the summer hadn't happened.

"I heard you went into hiding over the summer," Butch said. "But you can't run from your funeral."

If I was going to go to heaven, then the Good Lord had a welcome mat ready for me. But that wasn't my first choice.

"Leave me alone," I said.

Butch laughed and mocked me. "Lenny wants us to have mercy on him. Usually, you don't talk. It's better that way."

Everything morphed into slow motion as Butch reared back and threw a punch.

I channeled my training and imagined myself anywhere but in the path of Butch's fist.

Instantly, I materialized behind him. I tapped him on the shoulder. When he turned around, I punched *him* in the face.

"I told you to leave me alone!"

Butch toppled down in slow motion. It was so beautiful, angels should have been singing opera as he hit the ground face-first.

Butch lay on the ground, stunned.

"Get him!" he cried, pointing at me.

His cronies looked at each other in confusion. Then they shrugged and charged me.

I kept disappearing and punching them one by one until all the cronies lay on the floor groaning like beat-up bad guys in a Bruce Lee movie.

I didn't need to say anything else, so I just walked away.

I left Butch Stokes on the ground as an act of mercy. He never bothered me again.

When Mama came home that night, I was sitting on the carpet in front of the TV watching a rerun of *Sanford and Son*.

"How was your first day of school, baby?" she asked. She stopped and studied me, one eyebrow askew. "You didn't encounter Butch, did you? I don't see any scratches on you."

"I encountered him, all right," I said. "I did what Uncle Funky told me."

Mama put a hand on her hip and said, "Well, I'll be. There are such things as miracles."

She threw off her purse on the couch and kicked off her high heels. "I didn't bring you anything to eat because I was thinking we could go out to celebrate."

I crawled over to the television and turned down the volume. My mother and I *never* went out to eat. She barely made enough money to pay rent. If I got lucky, she brought me home something from the diner.

"But I thought we couldn't go out to eat, Mama," I said.

"I misspoke," she said, winking at me. "We don't need to go *out*. Maybe you ought to do what Funky told you. That thing about using your eyes."

I blinked, and the next thing I knew, our tiny little apartment wasn't an apartment anymore. It was an exquisite French restaurant. Golden chandeliers hung from the ceiling, and a duo of men in gray suits played a guitar and an accordion.

Our regular old kitchen table was replaced with a circular table with a red checkered cloth that had a spread of deli meats, snails, cheese, and a bottle of wine for Mama!

"Wait a minute," I said. "You mean—"

"Runs in the family. I thought it would be better if your uncle taught you, since he's the real master."

"You got that right!" said a voice.

Uncle Funky. On the table was my red radio with golden speakers. Uncle Funky was talking to us, clear as day.

"Tell me something good, Lenny."

I pulled out Mama's chair and helped her sit down as a lanky French waiter with a black vest and thin mustache strode out of a swinging door nearby, speaking French.

I laughed as I took my place at the table.

ALL HALLOWED ROADS

Camden was three miles away from the Village of the Forgotten when the mudslides hit. He was on his wagon, driving his horses ever further over the foggy mountain path when the ground rumbled and he saw the hills shake off their wig of trees and grass.

He watched spellbound as a great river of mud and debris poured down the mountainside toward the sea. He knelt and prayed a prayer of thankfulness for not being in the middle of it, for not being farther along in his journey. For he was not ready to meet the sea—not like this.

The mudslide had spooked his horses too, and it took all the strength he had to rein them in. A few times, he thought he'd lose them and he was certain that they were going to leave him stranded on the mountain with nothing but the clothes he was wearing.

But he calmed them without any loss.

He went as far as he could down the path before he reached the point where it washed out.

The dirt road was gone, and mud flowed over it, too thick to pass.

He climbed down from the wagon and cupped his hands to his eyes.

Was the village still there?

He couldn't see anything through the white fog—only the outlines of the firs and the rocks.

His stomach rumbled, half in pain and half in anxiety. Just hours before, he had been eating at a traveler's campfire. A chocolate pie. Two weak barley beers. A traveler, an old man with jewel-green eyes who cradled a copper mug with both hands, had leaned over and told him it would be wise if he stayed the night. Camden had asked him why, and the man changed the subject. He stayed and entertained the old man, a lackadaisical decision that he hated himself for at the time but was very glad for now.

But Camden had to make the delivery. It couldn't wait.

He peeked under the tarp of his wooden wagon; it was a bed of ore, dull-faced with glistening specks here and there.

What was a wagon full of ore if the buyers were dead?

He wiped his forehead with his flax shirt. Maybe he made a mistake in buying the ore. This wasn't his normal profession. He'd just been a poor farmer with an empty wagon, with no wife or child because the droughts had taken them a decade ago, an easy man for a stranger to make a proposition to.

It started to drizzle. First the rains were intermittent. Then they fell slowly and evenly across the mountain, thoroughly soaking him.

He had to get his horses somewhere dry. He climbed atop the wagon and took the reins. His horses turned around and backtracked.

He didn't want to go back to Hopewell, but he didn't have much of a choice. He was already miles from home. But he didn't like to spend the night among strangers, especially other travelers. He preferred to sleep under the open skies, alone, in the company of his animals.

But who knew if the rest of the mountain would give way? As far as he knew, he was in the danger zone.

He rode, listening to the rain pattering on the dirt path and his wagon as it cut grooves in the mud. He kept his ears open for any clues of another mudslide.

He was strategizing about how to deliver the shipment when a shadow flashed overhead, followed by a roar.

He held his breath. He debated turning off the road and hiding in the trees, but he wasn't fast enough.

"Human, what are you doing here?" a booming voice asked.

A serpentine dragon descended from the sky. It was twenty feet long, with dark blue scales covered in mud and a mouth full of serrated teeth.

It was a Crafter, the kind of dragon that shaped the land and traded with humans. Crafters were in tune with nature and often repaired the damage that magic-casting caused to the land. Camden sighed with relief that it wasn't a Keeper dragon —if it were, then he would have been dead. Crafters were known to be friendly—well, friendly wasn't the best word. *Reasonable.*

"You chose a bad time to travel," the dragon said.

"I wasn't planning on a mudslide today," Camden said.

The dragon landed on the path in front of him and coiled up like a snake. It reared its head back, its red, cabochon eyes glowing in the rain. "No one plans for a mudslide. Yet it is necessary."

Dragonspeak. They often spoke in strange non sequiturs, statements followed by mantras. Camden had heard that they did this to size you up, determine if you were a threat.

"Did you cause the mudslide?" Camden asked.

He had only met a few dragons in his lifetime, and the best way to engage with them was to dodge around their mantras and ask questions.

"The mudslide was necessary. I do not prefer to repeat myself."

"Why are they necessary?" Camden asked.

"There are elves in these parts. I'll have to repair this land for decades to fix the damage they've done."

"I'll have to travel for days to get around this mess."

The dragon's eyes narrowed as he saw Camden's wagon. "This isn't human territory—why are you here?"

"I'm just passing through."

Sensing the dragon was thinking about his wagon, he gestured to it and asked, "Any chance you can lend a hand?"

The dragon sniffed. "That depends on what you are transporting."

Camden gulped. Was this dragon in Lord Dark's regime? If it found out he was transporting ore, he could be accused of transporting contraband. He was trading with elves, and they were going to use the ore to manufacture magic. He didn't know that for sure, but it was the most obvious guess, given elves' untrustworthy history.

Trade between humans and elves didn't sit well with the Dragon Lord, and he had been taking brutal action to stop it. But for Camden, the payoff from the job and the allure of seeing more of the world was greater than the risk.

"It smells suspicious," the dragon said.

"I'm making a shipment," Camden said. "I hope you'll respect my buyer's cargo."

"Who is your buyer?"

"All I have is a location," Camden said, procuring a slip of paper. "I am just a driver."

The dragon peeled back the tarp and beheld the wagon full

of ore. He laughed a bone-shaking laugh that made Camden's heart race.

"You mined this ore?"

"No."

The dragon sniffed. "You smell like a farmer."

"You're right."

"Then how did you get it?"

"I picked it up from a seller."

"Who?"

"I prefer not to say."

"Then you prefer to die. You are aware of the Dragon Lord's laws?"

"Yes, except that the seller is a dragon."

The dragon cocked an eyebrow. He leaned in close and blew a cloud of smoke into Camden's face. Camden coughed and stepped back, swatting the smoke away.

"So a dragon put you up to this. Why didn't you say so?" He uncoiled and pointed his body toward the washed-out road. "Your deference is appreciated, as is your discretion."

Discretion?

He knew better than to ask.

Something didn't feel right, but he had no choice but to steer the horses back toward the washed-out road as the dragon flew above him.

When they arrived, the dragon dove into the river below and made a bridge out of his body.

Camden and the horses crossed.

"Thanks," Camden said as he made it to the other side.

"Proceed down the mountain to the village. If you need help, call. Do not delay, human."

The dragon flew into the sky and disappeared among the trees, roaring. Camden threw himself against the back of his seat and sighed.

God, he'd made it. He thought he was going to die for sure when the dragon saw the ore.

Luck had been on his side twice today already.

He drove the wagon down the mountain, and as he descended, the roads, wet and muddy, grew firmer.

The fog lifted. He heard birds' gentle calls—he had forgotten how quiet the surroundings got when dragons were near.

In a little while, he'd be at the beach. He had never been to the coast. His wife, Alina, had never been either. They were humble farmers living off the land in the center of the western continent. A man who grew wheat and soy had no use for the beach. But when the beetles infested the fields, and when the fields dried up, a man dreamed of fish to get him through.

There had been no fish either, not in those days. The elves kept it all to themselves, and they kept a stronghold on the coasts, using magical barriers to prevent anyone other than themselves from fishing.

Camden had watched his wife die in his arms from starvation. She was four months pregnant. Even though he gave her all his portions, even though he did everything he could to save her, it was not enough. He himself was days from death until the Dragon Lord took mercy on his village and delivered a wagon full of meat and vegetables.

Camden's neighbors had to force feed him. He had been angry that the food hadn't come sooner; the Dragon Lord knew of the famine and yet did nothing. He had been angry that he didn't die first. He had been angry that his heart, so full of grief, hadn't broken completely and let him die.

For better or worse, he survived. The farm meant nothing to him anymore, and he sold all his possessions and wandered the world in search of a better home.

And maybe that home was on the coast, where the air was cooler and the food more plentiful.

As he drove through the last of the firs and broke out into a steep valley overlooking the sea, his heart hurt for Alina.

The salty, piny air gathered on his tongue, and he took in a lung-full as his horses negotiated the steep path smoothly.

A constellation of twinkles on the shore caught his eye.

The village. It hadn't been washed away. As he rode down the mountain, he thought about all the things he would do with the two thousand spiras he'd been promised. That was two months' worth of crops, enough to get him through the spring. How far could he go? Far, far away from the western continent. He'd buy a few extra wagon parts, extra feed for the horses just in case. He could live off the land, and he could hunt. This was the beginning of a beautiful voyage.

He made it onto the sand, and the horses were more at ease the moment their hooves hit the sand. They pulled the wagon effortlessly across a brown beach as the waves crashed against the shore.

He looked at the blue horizon and grinned. A wooden boat was far out; a fisherman was onboard, and he pulled up a net full of flopping fish.

Camden approached a village of straw huts.

A group of men had been watching ever since he came out of the mountain pass. They were elven men, tall and unflinching and shirtless, with slightly pointed ears that were the only major difference between them and Camden, aside from their bright eyes. As Camden commanded his horses to stop, they went immediately to the back of the wagon and pulled back the tarp.

"Hey, a little courtesy would be nice," Camden said.

"We don't have time," one of the men said, carrying away as much ore as he could carry.

Camden felt a knot in his throat. How would he prove how much ore he had? He wanted to lasso the men and stop them from running away, but they walked quickly toward the mouth of a forest, and were gone.

"Don't worry," said an elderly voice. "You will be paid the correct sum."

A bald elf emerged from a hut with a leather pouch. From his stature, he looked like an elder.

"I am Anserin," the man said. "Welcome to our village." He tossed the pouch to Camden.

The pouch was heavier than it looked. Camden untied the strings and peeked at a sea of coins. It felt like two thousand spiras. It had the right amount of heft.

"Once you're done unloading, I'll be on my way," Camden said.

Thunder rumbled in the sky as storm clouds offshore moved in toward the beach. Anserin glanced up. "We're expecting storms tonight, and with the mudslides..."

Camden nodded. He wasn't going to neglect another elder's advice today. "I'll sleep on the beach," he said. "I'll find a place for my horses."

Anserin grinned. With a hand signal, an elven woman appeared almost out of nowhere and took Camden's horses. The horses let her lead—unusual because they only knew Camden's touch.

"Your horses will be fine," the old man said.

Camden could only watch as the girl in the plain white dress led the horses into the forest.

"Don't be alarmed," the elder said. "You can leave at dawn tomorrow."

Camden glanced around the beach. A group of elves were building a hut. A strong wave sprayed a blast of sea foam on them and they wiped water from their eyes. Nearby, several canoes bobbed at a pier.

"We are happy to offer you food if you're willing to work for it," Anserin said.

"I'm no stranger to work."

"Are you from the fields?"

"Central western."

"Then you understand the importance of a hard night's work."

Camden wasted no time. He took off his shirt and joined the men.

He grabbed a bundle of wheat lying in the sand. He knew that fragrant smell anywhere—that lightly toasted scent that made him a kid again, walking with his father through endless fields of wheat under a dull blue sky.

He climbed a wooden ladder to the top of the stone hut where an elf was perched on the roof, hammering a metal rod into a bundle of wheat, attaching it to the scaffolding.

Camden did the same, and the two worked silently yet understood each other, covering every inch of the roof with wheat. All the while, Camden climbed up and down the ladder, smoothing out the straw with a hammer, making sure it was sloped at just the right angle.

The wind picked up, blowing against the roof fiercely, but their work was solid. No part of the roof broke.

"Good work," the elf said as they climbed down the ladder. The elves shook his hand, and without a word, they loped into the forest.

Camden stared after them. To work side by side and never speak was foreign to him. Humans loved to talk. He wasn't much of a talker—not anymore—but he preferred the companionship of conversation. Or song. The experience left him empty, like after a Sunday morning prayer.

Anserin emerged from his hut and motioned to him.

Camden followed Anserin into the cool, dark hut. For an elder's hut, it was surprisingly spare—it had only runes scribbled in the sand and a small fire burning in the center of the floor. Camden wondered what the runes meant and what kind of magic Anserin knew.

They sat in the sand and Anserin offered him a star fruit.

"So this place is the Village of the Forgotten?" Camden asked. "Why do you call it that?"

"This village is not named after the past. It is named after the future."

Whatever that meant. Anserin answered so quickly and definitively that Camden thought it best not to press anymore.

"How long have you lived here?"

"A few weeks."

Weeks. That meant that this village had sprung up almost overnight. It also meant that it didn't exist when he started his journey. Elves weren't known to be nomadic. To build a village so suddenly was odd, but not out of the ordinary. Every village had to have a start.

Camden thought of his own farm. Would he have been suspicious of a farmer who set up in empty land and started using it? No, he thought. Live and let live.

The elven girl entered the hut and brought in a wooden plate with an entire fish—a tilapia, the head still on, garnished with dill and roasted corn. Camden guessed from her looks that she was in her early twenties. She was the same girl who had taken his horse. She had long, brown hair. She avoided his gaze.

"Where did you get the corn?" Camden asked, digging into the fish with his fingers.

"We have our ways," Anserin said. "You may sleep in my hut. You have paid the cost of your meal and stay. We will reunite you with your possessions before first light."

The elven girl left and returned again. She carried a bundle of straw and made him a bed in the center of the hut so that he could lie with his feet to the fire.

Anserin stood and gave Camden a half bow. "Make yourself comfortable."

The girl bowed and exited after Anserin.

Camden lay on the straw and took off his boots. He didn't know how to make himself comfortable in an elven village.

Yet it was easy to rest his head on the straw and gaze out the window as the rain fell across the beach.

Thunder rocked the hut for several hours with its insistent growling, and as the storm died, he drifted off.

Sometime between sleep and waking, the elven girl entered again. She knelt in front of his bed.

"Is everything okay?" Camden asked.

She put a finger to his lips and crawled in with him.

"Listen, I'm not—"

She embraced him. He resisted her, but she hugged him so tightly that he could not push her away.

She rested her head against his bare chest. Her long hair brushed against his skin. She looked up at him with her bright green eyes. Her hands wandered downward, and downward and—

He grabbed her by the wrist and shook his head.

"I'm sorry," he said.

But she did not leave him. She lay in the bed, in his arms. And she cried.

In the middle of the night, he woke to chanting outside.

The girl was gone. Her side of the bed was cold. His eyes burned and he wiped sleep from them. The chanting was quiet, like an out-of-tune hymn.

He pushed aside the straw curtain and went outside, where a group of elves were gathered on the beach. They stood in concentric circles, holding hands.

They sang:

Smile for us, old dragon lord,

for the world may soon stop spinning. Shadow's flame is you, old lord,

and this dead world needs your kindling.

Something wasn't adding up. A pang struck Camden's stomach and he was going to be sick.

He uttered a curse. He charged across the beach and found Anserin. The bald elder sang laughing a mad laugh with his hands outstretched.

Camden grabbed him by the shoulder and spun him around.

When the old man opened his eyes, Camden punched him in the jaw, and the man collapsed into the sand with his hands over his face.

"You want to tell me what the hell is really going on?"

"It's too late."

"What do you mean 'too late'?"

Anserin wiped away a spot of blood. "We've tried to make your stay comfortable. We've given you the opportunity for industry, a good meal, and a restful sleep by the sea. You refused one of our women."

"I want my horses."

"You will be reconnected with your possessions before first light—"

"No. *Now.*"

The elves whispered amongst themselves.

"You cannot leave," Anserin said quietly.

Camden shrank back.

Anserin pulled himself to his feet, and two men steadied him. "Soon, the Dragon Lord will arrive. And we will fight him."

"I'll be gone before then." Camden glanced toward the forest and tried to figure out where his horses were.

"I have lied to you. Your horses are dead. We showed you such hospitality because you, like us, stand on the verge of life and death, and we wanted to calm you before the battle. No one will leave this place until victory is won. We may be the Village of the Forgotten, but we will not die in failure. Word of our plans cannot spread. As I said, we tried to make you comfortable. We needed the ore to fuel our magical assault, and we thank you for that. But you will not be leaving."

Several roars filled the sky. In the distance, a fleet of shapes flickered against the clouds.

Dragons.

"Dear god—"

He couldn't be seen among resistance. It was grounds for instant death.

Camden dashed for the forest.

A leg tripped him. He crashed face first in the sand.

Elves scattered out of the huts as the shadows approached.

"As we planned!" Anserin cried. "Be ever stoic! Do not show emotion! We will surprise them when they least expect it."

In the sky, a loud voice yelled: "You are in the presence of the Dragon Lord. Prostrate yourselves."

The dragons approached in a V formation. A larger shape was in the center, and Camden could see its green eyes glowing from far away.

It was him, the Dragon Lord, the one responsible for Alina's death. Even if Camden had a sword, it wouldn't have given him the courage he needed. His legs gave way and he fell to his knees.

"Rejoice, human," Anserin said. "For the Dragon Lord will die tonight. And you will have your freedom."

"What do I care?" Camden asked quietly.

"The Dragon Lord killed your wife, did he not?"

Camden was silent for a while. "How did you know that?"

"You are a wanderer in search of meaning, are you not?"

A dragon descended from the sky. It was the serpentine dragon from the mountain.

"Sing for the Dragon Lord," the dragon cried.

"As we rehearsed!" Anserin said, raising his hands to direct the chant.

The elves sang, and Camden couldn't think as they chanted out-of-tune as loudly as they could.

He could only close his eyes as the fleet of dragons descended on the beach. He fell forward, buried his face in the sand and gave up.

The next morning, waves washed on the shore of the Village of the Forgotten just the same.

Across the dozens of bodies lying face down. No survivors.

Across the pools of blood and flags with runes staked in the sand. Even across the piles of ore overturned at the forest's edge.

The serpentine dragon raked up the casualties with his long tail. These elves were useful pawns. Their deaths were planned, though they themselves thought they had a chance at survival.

He paused to look up at the mountains.

The mudslides had worked. They had stopped all armies from marching to the Dragon Lord's defense.

For the Dragon Lord was dead now, and the Village of the Forgotten would soon be forgotten. There was a new Dragon Lord now.

The serpentine dragon grinned. He, a humble Crafter from the mountains who played a key role in the betrayal of the old lord, would be the new lord's right hand.

He stacked the bodies on top of one another, and he blew fire on them to start the burning. The smell of searing flesh invigorated him.

He continued dragging his tail across the sand, slow, ragged, like a plow tilling soil...

His tail dredged up a body. Camden.

The dragon took the body in his hands and searched it until it found the leather pouch full of coins.

He held Camden's broken body in his claws. He remembered the man's simple history, the cautiousness, the deference, and the respect, the only bright spot among this band of elves.

He regarded the body for a time. Then, instead of throwing it onto the pyre, he flung it into the sea.

RETURN TO EXODUS RANCH

When Milo Candlesea parked in the driveway of his family ranch, it looked the same as it always had—a three-story brick house with the sea behind it. Just over the water, the metropolitan skyline of Magic Hope City rose in the distance, impossibly far away but always a whisper in the air.

He stepped out of a black, government-issue car and shook his head at the house.

The shutters had collapsed into the grass, riddled with bullet holes. No window had been spared. One of the rooms on the third floor had been scorched from a fire, and looked like a burnt eyelid.

A swing on the porch creaked in the wind, and somewhere, a cow lowed.

He walked through the dead brown grass, up a set of wooden stairs to the porch. A tea set jangled on a wireframe table as he walked across the porch. The glasses still had dribbles of sun tea in them, as if the drinkers would be right back.

He had sat on this porch many nights with his mother, talking about their lineage: how the elven world used to be, and how it wasn't anymore on account of the alliance between humans and dragons, and how there was a lot to be ashamed of in this era of magical technology.

He reached a pair of red double doors with a brass door knocker shaped like a fish. A pentagram glowed warmly in the center of the doors, a mix of pink, purple, and green.

His family insignia.

He hadn't seen it in years. Not since he joined the militia. These doors were the last thing he'd seen after his father slammed them in his face, yelled that he had betrayed his lineage by going to Magic Hope City, and then, to the wars on the eastern continent. As he drove away, Milo had kept staring at the doors in the rearview mirror, hoping that they would open, that his mother and father would come running for him with their arms outstretched to give him a proper goodbye fit for a soldier.

But the doors never opened. Instead, a magical wall had sprung up around the house, an impenetrable purple spell that Milo knew would keep him out until his father had a change of heart or was dead.

So he kept driving, into the future, into the depths of blood and war. He managed to survive the magical wars, though the images of dragons, gunfire and gruesome deaths at the hands of vicious spells would never leave him.

Now he was here, and aside from the damage to the home, it was as if he'd never left.

A car door shut behind him. A silver-haired man in fatigues and sunglasses leaned against the car. He had pointed ears and orange, jewel-like eyes that glimmered underneath the sunglasses.

"We did what we could," Wizenberry said. He was the head of the Magic Hope Guard, the one who commanded the response to the home. "But they didn't leave us much of a choice."

Milo turned his head but did not look at Wizenberry. "I imagine they gave you a fight."

"Like you wouldn't believe. Your parents were tough. I still can't understand why they did it, though."

Milo didn't feel like answering the question. "What am I going to find in here?"

Wizenberry shrugged. "This whole place was sealed with a spell before they died. No one's been inside since...the exodus. The bodies are gone, so don't worry about that. We figured since your tour was over and you're the last surviving blood relative, that—"

"Thanks, but I don't have any intention of helping the army anymore. My service is done."

"Can you at least take a look around and tell me what you think?"

Milo put his hand on the pentagram and it pulsed at his touch, shimmered, and disappeared. The doors unlocked, and he pushed them open.

The house was in tatters. The foyer was lined with family photos—Milo and his seventeen brothers and sisters. The frames lay on the floor in a flood of broken glass.

All of his siblings were dead. These might have been the only remnants left of their existence aside from the government records. He told himself he'd come back for the photos after he finished walking around. But he wondered if he really wanted to remember them.

As they made their way through an oak-paneled hallway, they stepped around broken furniture and trash.

He stopped at a photo of him and his father—a tall, balding man in a purple suit and polka-dotted ascot, with high cheekbones like Milo's and a stately air. He and Milo stood unsmiling in a black and white photo. His father never smiled, never showed emotion except anger.

Wizenberry stopped at the photo and put his hands behind his back, studying it like a painting in a museum.

"What was it like having a father as an Elder?" he asked.

Wizenberry wasn't pure blood. Decades ago, one of his ancestors had lain with a human. Anyone with less than one hundred percent elven blood was excluded from the inner circles of elven society, an ancient custom that Milo never agreed with, but that his parents observed strictly. But aside from his skin and manner of speaking, Wizenberry looked no different than Milo.

"My father was a strict man," Milo said. "He believed in the values of another time."

"Always wondered what it would be like, you know. To sit around a table, light candles, and sing spells, like they used to do. These days, you just buy spells at the store, use 'em up, and they're gone. There's something romantic about all this."

Wizenberry grabbed a candle with a burnt-out wick and twirled it between his fingers. "When your parents made the announcement to the media, they sent me and some troops. We had to cut off all utility services to the house."

Milo nodded. Made sense. There were more candles about than normal.

"That wouldn't have fazed them," Milo said.

"It didn't."

They continued into the living room, where a maze of sleeping bags lay across the floor amidst dirty plates of eaten food. There were stacks of old books everywhere, and Milo recognized them from his father's library. The air was musty, as if body odors had lingered for several weeks.

Wizenberry looked as if he'd had a revelation. "I get it now. There are a lot of sleeping bags."

"So?"

"We were wondering where they kept the children."

Milo grimaced. That there had been children in the house wouldn't have normally saddened him, but that so many of them were his nieces and nephews...

"I've been to other exodus ranches," Wizenberry said. "The one thing that gives me consolation is that whatever they did, however, they did it, there are never any bodies. Thank goodness for that."

Milo knelt and reached into a sleeping bag. He pulled out a stuffed dragon with a torn wing.

It had been his eight-year-old niece's. He remembered her laughing face, her flowing black hair, how she begged him not to go. She was young enough to know about the religious rules and still not care. Or maybe it was because his rebellious spirit rubbed off on her. He'd held her in his arms while his parents watched grim-faced. His brother refused to make eye contact with him.

He balled the dragon and threw it against the wall. His hands trembled and it took everything he had to stop from breaking down.

Wizenberry sensed Milo's sadness and went ahead into the kitchen. "Wow."

Milo pulled himself together and welcomed the distraction. He joined Wizenberry in the large, elegant kitchen with a granite island in the center and wallpaper decorated with fish. The door to the pantry was open, and inside, a ladder leading down into a food bunker.

"How much food did they have?"

"More than you'd think. Last I heard, my mother had enough food to support fifty people for two years."

His mother knew how to can. Fish. Oysters. Vegetables that she and his sisters grew on the farm, just like his ancestors had done. All these years later, some things never changed.

He picked up a tin can that held half a sardine. He ignored the putrid smell as he threw it into a trash can. "Another elven thing you probably didn't know we could do."

"Canning? Come on. The stockpiling? No, totally blew me away."

They stood at a sliding patio door that opened onto a beach. Stormy gray waves washed ashore, pushing and pulling cans of food and trash across the sand.

"They held out for a month," Wizenberry said. "Long enough for travelers to arrive from all over the continent. It killed me to see it. Hordes and hordes of elves showed up with food and as many personal belongings as they could carry. And they walked right through the purple wall in front of the ranch. There wasn't a damn thing that I could do about it. Talk about a strong spell. I can't tell you how much ammunition we fired into it, how many counter spells we tried."

"Don't be so hard on yourself."

"After a month, the number of newcomers each day decreased. And when it hit zero, that's when we started to get scared."

"How many days total was it?"

"Thirty-six."

Milo puffed. Thirty-six. The holy number. Over a century ago, a group of elven villagers banded together to overthrow a Dragon Lord. There were thirty-six villagers, and the plan, from start to finish, lasted thirty-six days. When the Dragon Lord fell, it ushered in the birth of their religion.

He hated the significance. He hated that it gave his parents justification for what they did.

Milo turned and put a hand on Wizenberry's shoulder. "I don't blame you for this."

Wizenberry had an afflicted look, as if he carried the weight of that fateful night with him. "If you don't blame me yet, you will."

They walked outside, across the beach, to a large, gray barn with the family pentagram burned onto the shingled roof.

Wizenberry pulled the doors open, and they entered.

"This is where it happened."

Milo smelled hay and a burning, astringent smell that he couldn't place.

Wizenberry stood in the center of the barn. "Your parents would have been right here. Your siblings and family would have stood around them. And the visitors, around them in concentric circles. There were so many that they didn't fit in the barn; the fields were full." He pointed to a white speaker on the side of the barn. "Your father prayed into the speakers so that all could hear."

Wizenberry reached into his pocket and unfolded a sheet of paper. Milo read it.

Be it known today that we, the elven race, do not agree with the alliance between humans, dragons, and elves. We especially do not agree with those of our race who have disavowed tradition.

The world needs us, but because it has chosen to ignore our warnings about the dragon race, we instead choose to disappear...

Milo handed the paper back. His father had written it. The words were spoken like a true Elder.

"All of this seems like a dream, still," Milo said. "I can't believe that I'm one of the only purebloods left."

"You're not the only one. There are others like you, others who are more reasonable about the state of the world."

"How many?"

"A couple hundred maybe. If that. Compared to a couple

hundred thousand that died. This wasn't the only exodus ranch."

They left the barn, and Wizenberry whistled to the driveway.

Several large, black vans had parked in the grass near the house. Soldiers exited the cars, and they helped out families of elves.

He watched as the elves gathered in a line and made their way through the fields, looking around nervously. There were at least a hundred of them—men, women, children and babies. All with pointed ears, bright eyes, jewel-toned clothing and the classic stoic look that Milo recognized in his own people.

"I hope you don't mind," Wizenberry said.

Jerk move. Of course Milo minded, but what was he going to say? "I told you that I'm not going to—"

"Sorry, Milo, to ask you to do this at the last minute. But isn't spontaneity one of the tenets of our religion?"

"My religion."

Wizenberry looked offended. "This is coming down from the governor. It's not me. You're not a soldier anymore. What else did you plan to do with your life?"

His tone made Milo uneasy.

"Sergeant, what exactly do you want me to do?"

"We need you to be the next Elder of the western continent."

"This wasn't in my runes."

"And you think it was in your dad's?"

Wizenberry blocked him from escaping. His hands were on his hips, inches from his holster. "I know all about your dad and how he stole the Eldership."

It was true. His father had cheated a woman out of the position. But she wasn't fit for it; it was in her runes, but her heart wasn't in it. At least that was what Milo believed.

"Is there no one else willing to do the job?"

"Oh, there are plenty, but you're the one the governor wants."

"Why?"

"You have military experience. You're loyal to the government. You haven't made any major dragon enemies."

"I don't want this."

Wizenberry pulled out another sheet of paper. On it was a conscription order with Milo's name on it.

"I've already served. You can't draft me again."

"There are no laws against it. Milo, we need someone like you. Just a few years as an Elder and you can do whatever you want. Retire. Consult. We don't care. As long as you get us results."

"I have a life," Milo said, pointing his finger in Wizenberry's face, "and for the last three years of it, I've given it to the militia."

"And we appreciate your service. But you're not done yet." The line of elves made it to the barn.

Wizenberry climbed up on a platform next to the barn. He clapped his hands to get everyone's attention.

"Listen up. You all are the last survivors of the pure elven race," he said. "Look around. This is what's left of your people."

Silence. Everyone looked around, at each other.

"You folks are the last people who can channel pure magic," Wizenberry said. "Our entire society was built on the back of magic. When you go, so does our magic. So it is now your responsibility, whether you like it or not, to figure out a way we're going to sustain our magic supply. Oh, and we need a photo. It's for historical purposes."

Photo flashes went off as several soldiers took pictures of the group.

"What do you think you're doing?" Milo asked. "They deserve to mourn in peace."

"Spoken like an Elder."

"I thought you had respect for your lineage."

"Too much," Wizenberry said. "And I'm not going to watch it fade away." Wizenberry walked away and waved as the other soldiers joined him. "Oh, and by the way—" Wizenberry said.

A purple wall sprang up around the ranch. It glowed like a cascading waterfall, and Wizenberry and the other soldiers watched in awe.

Milo ran to the wall, but it repelled him. It knocked him thirty feet, and he landed on his back. Several elves helped him up.

"Wizenberry, you son of a—"

"I need a strategy from you. I'll be back tomorrow, Elder Candlesea."

The soldiers got into their cars and drove away, kicking up clouds of dust as they sped down the gravel road.

Milo tried to gather his thoughts. The other elves whispered. "What just happened?"

"Are we trapped?"

All eyes looked to Milo. He didn't know what to say.

An older man stepped forward. He had a triangular face and wore a black button-up shirt. His eyes looked like they were slanted shut. He had a lion's mane of gray hair, and a paunch. "If they trapped us, then that means they want a fight."

"Stop," Milo said. "They're not looking for violence."

"They're not, are they? Then why'd they lock us up, the last remaining pure bloods, inside of a confinement spell? They think that because the rest of our idiotic race decided to kill themselves, that maybe we have violent propensities too."

"They want us to kill ourselves!" someone shouted.

"We need an Elder!" another woman cried.

"That will be me," the older man said. "I, Castor Grimoire, will be the Elder of this place. I was second-in-line back home and---"

The elves spoke over each other.

"Elders don't just appoint themselves," a woman said. "We have to vote, don't we?"

"I thought we drew straws. Elders are picked by fate."

"Well, what if fate doesn't cooperate?"

"This is an emergency," Castor said. "And we need someone who is unwilling to compromise, a man who—"

"Why does it have to be a man?" someone asked.

Castor flushed.

Milo's head throbbed amidst the chatter and the arguments.

He thought about going back to war and maybe it was the best option.

But going to war meant he would surely die. And he didn't want to die. He didn't want to join his parents and brothers and sisters in death. He glanced back to the ranch, then at the wall.

He climbed atop the platform next to the barn and whistled. The group quieted, looking up at him.

"We are not going to debase our own blood," Milo said. He felt his father's spirit with him as he spoke, and he hated it.

"I am Milo Candlesea. Viator Candlesea was my father, and this was his farm."

He tried not to let the frightened eyes scare him.

"I never asked for any of this, and neither did any of you. We are all here today because we chose to live. And whatever that means...I-I guess we have to figure that out."

Confidence took hold in the group and he found supportive looks from a family in the front row. He focused on them, stammering as he started again.

"We can do this the way our ancestors did it or we can throw the tradition in the sea. It doesn't matter to me. But either way, the government is not going to let us out until we unify." He pointed to the house. "My mother canned enough food in there for all of us."

A woman with a baby joined him on the platform. She had curly hair and wore a blouse with spaghetti straps, as if she had left her home in a hurry. The baby, wrapped in teal blankets in her arms, began to cry. She rocked him gently. "He's right. We are only as strong as our agreement."

Castor Grimoire folded his arms. "And why should we trust you? Your father put us in this mess."

"I say we move for a vote," Milo said, ignoring him. "By show of hands. In twenty-four hours, if you're dissatisfied with my leadership, I'll step down and you can vote again. But I am the son of an Elder, I just toured in the war, and I know what the government wants from us. I'll get us out of here."

"Now hold on!" Castor yelled. "We need to talk about this more."

"I second Milo's motion," the woman said.

The hands went up. Milo won by twenty.

As several elves followed him to the house so that they could gather supplies for dinner, Milo felt weak and had no idea what to do.

Night fell on the ranch.

Milo piled all his father's books in the study. He went through them one by one, learning the customs of an Elder.

He tried the lights, but Wizenberry, true to his word, had kept the utilities to the house shut off so he had to read by candlelight.

He was familiar with most of the customs. He grew up in them. Like how an Elder was always the first and last to speak, how no one could speak against him unless they had a factual basis to do so.

But some of the Elder secrets made sense to him after so many years of wondering.

An Elder is the physical, emotional and spiritual leader of the community.

He must always stand upright.

He must always keep hold of his emotions, for the community will mirror him, and even in the face of disaster, they must mirror calmness, like the face of placid water.

He must stand for what he believes in, even if there is a chance he could be wrong.

He must stand for action, even if decisions are made in haste.

He must swear to uphold the elven way of life, even if drastic measures need to be taken.

He saw his father in the tenets. Milo imagined him, locked in his study, among candlelight, books and a solitary glass of water, with his hands over his head.

What would his father do in this situation?

That much was clear.

His mother?

He thought of Wizenberry. And Castor. The governor, in a gray building somewhere moving him across a war map like a chess piece.

At every turn, someone wanted to see him fail.

Someone knocked.

He peeped outside. It was the woman from before. The baby was asleep in her arms.

"I'm Cara, by the way," she said. "I heard you pacing. I would offer you a drink, but it's time."

Milo sighed. "Right."

"What's your plan?"

"I don't know yet."

Cara's eyes flashed with worry.

Milo craned his head to look at the baby. "Is he sleeping okay?"

"Not since his father died."

"Did he die...here?"

She lowered her eyes. "No. In the wars."

"I'm sorry."

"He was a human."

He glanced again at the baby. What a tough life that child would have.

He should have turned her away.

He should have told her that her life was now her own, and that there was no one she could depend on.

That was what the scripture said. It was what his father would have said. But instead, he said, "Let's go."

As they walked to the barn, he caught a glimpse of Magic Hope City between clusters of clouds.

He knew what he had to do.

They gathered in the barn. Milo ordered them to set up candles all over so that they could see each other, for there was little daylight left.

He sat in the middle of the barn with a book in his lap. Everyone sat at his command, and he still couldn't believe the power they had entrusted him with.

Everyone huddled in so close they could feel each other's breath, and the candle warmth radiated through the crowd.

"The government wants us to come up with a plan on how to protect the world's magic supply," he said. "And honestly, I can't blame them. We are the last of our blood. Not all of us are going to have children. Some of us...may choose to have children with humans, or with other elves who are believers in a new way."

He expected murmurs, but he had their attention.

"The government is scared. Only elves and dragons can channel magic, and dragons cannot be trusted. If we die out, so will magical society."

He stood. "I will never agree with what my father did, but this ranch is an exodus point."

Castor, in a rare gesture of deference, raised his hand and Milo pointed to him.

"So you're telling me we are going to kill ourselves?"

"No," Milo said. "We're going to live."

They spent all night tearing the barns on the ranch down, carrying timber by firelight to the sea. They repurposed the nails and screws they could find and used them to fasten the timber together into crude boats that Milo had learned to build when he was just a boy.

The ancient elven fishing boat, powered by oar, light upon the waves. They packed cans of fish onto the boats.

For a moment, Milo felt as if he had been transported back into time, to an age where all that mattered was your hard work. His muscles ached as he nailed the boats together, and he ran up and down the beach with the children, carrying as many tins of fish as he could without tripping.

Castor and a group of dissenters refused to participate; they sat on a hill overlooking the beach, watching grimly.

When the government cars arrived in the morning, and the purple wall shattered, Milo was ready for them.

He stood on the bow of a boat with an oar in his hand. All around him, an entire fleet of fishing boats bobbed in the ocean waves, ready to embark, the other elves waiting for his command.

Milo watched as Wizenberry stomped onto the sand. Behind him, a cavalry of black cars idled in the driveway, including a large limousine with blinking lights on its roof.

"What do you think this is?" Wizenberry asked.

"This is your answer," Milo said, gesturing to the boats with both of his hands.

"What we asked of you was simple," Wizenberry said. "You're making a fool of yourself. The governor is here!"

He pointed back to the line of cars frantically. He looked at Milo, breathing heavily.

"The governor is your problem now, Wizenberry."

The soldier pulled out his gun. Several of the elves in Milo's boat gasped.

Milo stood his ground. "You said you wanted a solution to the magic shortage," he said. "You kill us, you kill the world."

Wizenberry cocked his gun.

He and Milo stared each other down.

Wizenberry's finger trembled on the trigger. His arm shook. Milo didn't flinch.

Wizenberry fired. Milo closed his eyes.

There were screams. The sound of the ocean waves. The fierce wind ripping across his cheek.

Milo felt calmness spread over him.

This must have been what it felt like to die. All those years in the war, only to die like this...

He opened his eyes, expecting a hole in his chest. But there was no hole.

He expected someone else to be floating face down in the ocean waves, blood drifting across the waters.

But no one had fallen.

On the beach, Wizenberry knelt in the sand, clutching a knee. An arc of blood had spilled across the sand.

"It was a protection spell!" one of the elves cried.

Cara put her hand on her heart. "But we didn't cast any spells." She looked into the sky and smiled.

They hadn't cast any spells at all. The boats had been as unprotected as Milo, and he could not think of an explanation other than that it was a miracle. Suddenly, his father's stern face flashed across his mind's eye. A smirk spread across the old man's face. Milo shook it away.

Wizenberry screamed, and several soldiers charged through the grass and slid to his aid. Castor joined them.

"You're going to pay for this!" he shouted. "Just because you're pure blood doesn't mean you're better than us!"

One of the elves on Milo's boat pushed off, and the rest of the boats followed.

"We will find a solution," Milo said. "But we will do it in freedom." He pointed to Wizenberry with the oar and looked the soldier in the eye. "But if you come after me or anyone in my community here, I'll kill you myself, and I'll do it without magic."

Wizenberry's face hardened as the boats pulled away. Soon, the beach grew smaller and smaller as the boats sliced through the morning waves.

"Where will we go?" Cara asked.

Milo shook his head. "We're going home. Wherever that will be."

The sea pulled them into its broad depths as a storm brewed. They covered themselves with ponchos, said a prayer, and as the rain began to fall, they shared a meal of canned fish.

ALONE IN NAKED GREED

I van Little was so sick of picking up trash; he needed a hamburger.

He had signed up for the city's annual Earth Day Trash Fest, an afternoon where thousands of people gathered, put on bandanas and safety vests, and took to the downtown streets, picking up every cigarette butt and piece of garbage they could find.

He signed up because he got a free day off work, a call center downtown that was more like a jungle than an office. Any excuse to get out of that place was enough for him. He wouldn't have to listen to "coaching" from his boss or "motivational speeches" from the director or any of that other crap that made him roll his eyes so much, his eyeballs hurt.

Today, it was just the skies and the open outdoors.

Ivan was going to be an executive someday; but for now, he picked up trash with a silver trash grabber, stuffing it into a big plastic bag that ruffled in the wind.

He was randomly assigned to a group of people from an insurance company. Underwriters, he thought. Young. They all looked so happy, making jokes and playing music from a Bluetooth speaker as they made their way up the grassy median on Martin Luther King Boulevard.

He stuffed butt after butt into his silver bag, grumbling to himself.

He didn't care if people smoked, but it wasn't right that he had to be out here because they couldn't use a trash can.

Oh well, he told himself. Only three more hours and he'd be able to go home and play games online.

Then it hit him.

A waterfall in his loins.

The drip-drip.

A ball-like pressure in his crotch.

He had to pee.

He checked his watch, then he pulled out the glossy map he had kept rolled up in his back pocket. There were no portable toilets on his route. And he was in the median so he couldn't unzip his jeans and go in the grass.

He waved to the group leader, a blonde-haired woman who wore a baseball cap over her bandana.

"Hey, any chance I can take a break?"

"We really should keep going," the woman said. "There are portable toilets at Hill Square. And food."

Ivan said nothing.

Heaven forbid *she* had to go to the bathroom. He guaranteed she would have stopped the whole group to announce that she had to take a break.

It was bullshit.

He started ignoring the trash. He only picked up every other butt now. He decided to hold it a bit longer; city workers drove by every fifteen minutes to check on them. Maybe one of the workers could drive him up to Hill Square and back.

They crossed the street and came to a wooded area with

railroad tracks running through it. All the trees and shrubs were dead and there was trash everywhere.

Ivan had passed this area every morning, but he never realized how much trash there truly was.

"Look, there are blankets," someone said, pointing to a blanket tent wavering in the breeze.

"I'm not disturbing anybody's house," Ivan said, sidestepping around a condom. "You're probably liable to find a mobile meth lab in there."

He had seen those in the orientation. Coke bottles filled with sudsy, dirt-like liquid. They could blow up in your face.

To hell with that.

But just over the tips of the trees, he saw a beautiful sight: Freddy's Burgers. A neon sign of a black man in a suit and a feather in his cap glittered in the daylight. He sensed the faint whiff of burgers and fries.

Thick steak burgers. He'd eaten there plenty of times. He forgot it was on the route.

His stomach rumbled and he had to pee even more.

"Well, seeing as this area is slightly off the route," the supervisor said, "let's keep going."

"Actually," Ivan said, "I'll pick up a few items in there. Just the big ones you can see from the street."

"Too dangerous, Ivan," the supervisor said.

"I can do it. I'll be out once my bag is full." He faked a smile. "We've got to win the Biggest Butt contest, don't we?"

The "Biggest Butt" contest was a game between all the groups. Whoever found the most cigarette butts got free gift cards. To Ivan, it was complete and utter crap, but if his time in the call center taught him anything, it was that being enthusiastic about stupid stuff took you places.

The supervisor studied the wooded area with a look of

concern. Then she smiled back. "Okay. Thanks for your enthusiasm and willingness to go the extra mile!"

Ivan grinned at them until they started up the road.

He lingered behind, and as the group drifted further up the road, he dashed into the woods.

He took off his safety vest and draped it on a dead branch. He threw his trash bag and grabber on the ground and stalked through the woods with his hands in his pockets.

In a few minutes, he'd be in air-conditioned bliss with a hamburger in his hands...after he relieved himself, of course.

He passed the blanket tent and he heard something shift.

He stopped. His heart beat quickly. He sensed someone.

A shoe stuck out of the blankets. He hadn't seen it before.

A man with an unruly, almost Biblical beard crawled out of the tent. He wore a faded green army jacket and a worn knitted stocking cap. His pink t-shirt underneath was stained and had several holes in it.

"Hey, man, you wouldn't mind sparing me a little bit of change, would you?"

Ivan walked past him and didn't make eye contact.

Why don't you try picking up some of your trash first, Ivan thought. He patted his wallet to make sure it was still there, then climbed the grassy green hill toward the back entrance of Freddy's.

Maya Santos had been working the cash register at Freddy's all morning. It was almost the end of her shift, and she was grateful for it.

Her nails were starting to fade and her feet were tired.

Today was payday.

She'd already spent the money. She had a date with her

boyfriend, who was finishing up detasseling corn right about now. They were going to see a romance movie. Maybe he was going to propose.

The afternoon had been busier than normal with all the Earth Day celebrations. There had been so many people that the fryers never stopped, and the place smelled like burgers, spicy chicken, and French fries.

Usually, she could get the smell off herself when she showered. Today, she wasn't so sure.

A young man with a messy mop of black hair rushed into the restaurant and looked around frantically. He had such a worried look on his face that she thought he was going to have a panic attack.

He beelined for the bathroom and slammed the door behind him.

She shrugged.

Customers. They were so weird sometimes. Especially downtown. She'd asked to be transferred to the west side, closer to home, but she was a top performer and the district manager wouldn't hear it. ("Keep it up and you'll be me someday.")

At least the weird guy wasn't one of the Earth Day volunteers trying to use the bathroom without buying anything. She'd had to yell at a few people already today. Not because she wanted to, but because Freddy, the owner, would yell at her twice as bad if she didn't.

After all, they were running a business.

She leaned against the cash register and stared blankly at the screen as the man emerged from the bathroom, wiping his hands on his jeans.

He approached the register, his eyes wandering up to the screen. He looked like the cocky type once you got to know him.

She spoke as if a robot took control of her vocal cords.

"Welcome to Freddy's, home of the big fat steak burger. What can I do for you?"

The young man paused, then sighed as he tried to decide what he wanted.

"The chicken tender meal is selling like crazy today," she said, trying to help him. A line was starting to gather behind him.

"Nah, I think I'll just go for the burger."

She gave him the amount and he swiped his debit card. The card made a thin cracking sound as he passed it through the reader.

Her terminal beeped.

Declined.

"What?" the man asked. "I got paid yesterday."

"Well, your card is out of money," Maya said. "Got another one?"

The young man cursed and patted his pockets. He pulled out some cash and rifled through it. He glanced at the money in his palm and then up at the screen.

"I've only got five dollars and twenty cents."

"The total is six dollars and twenty cents."

"I work at the call center. Can you work with me? I'll bring you a dollar tonight."

She had a dollar in her pocket.

The last time she "paid" for someone, they never came back. How many times had she heard that excuse?

"Next customer, please," she said.

The young man trudged out of the restaurant with a dejected look in his eyes.

Maya rang up another customer and thought about being in her boyfriend's arms.

Ivan kicked a piece of trash across the sidewalk. The outside of Freddy's smelled like fresh burgers, and the smell seemed to taunt him, as if to say, 'You can't have me.'

His stupid debit card! Now he had to call the bank when he got home and wait on the line forever to make sure he wasn't a victim of fraud.

And that stupid cashier!

What did he look like, a bum? He'd been in there a million times. Added up, the money he spent at Freddy's probably paid her salary for a few months.

And he got booted out because of a dollar.

Freddy's could have afforded a dollar. If they couldn't, then that wasn't Ivan's problem.

A couple exited the restaurant with burgers in hand, biting into them.

Ivan looked away.

The feeling of anger subsided and he calmed down.

At least he'd gotten to use the bathroom.

He started back toward the woods.

As he walked, he thought about the homeless guy. Would he still be there? He might not be so friendly next time.

But the blanket tent was gone, and it was as if the homeless guy had never been there.

Ivan pushed through the trees and saw his safety vest fluttering in the wind.

It was ripped to shreds.

His trash grabber was snapped in half. His trash bag was ripped and its guts spilled out over the ground. The area smelled like fresh urine.

He scowled.

The bastard!

No point touching any of it now.

He walked onto the grass on the side of the road, to the area where he should have been picking up trash.

The rest of the crew was nowhere to be found. The grass, trashless and green, almost sparkled in the afternoon light. Nearby, large bags of trash sat on the curb.

Ivan sighed. Where had the group gone?

He walked down the side of the road, muttering to himself.

He just didn't have any luck today.

Forty-five minutes later, he made it to Hill Square, the bustling grounds of an office building where hundreds of people sat at plastic tables eating hot dogs.

A guitar player played folksy music on a stage.

The smell of food welcomed him, and he was grateful.

On the way to the food line, he encountered the team. They had just finished their meals and they looked at him like he was a man risen from the dead.

"Where did you go?" the supervisor asked.

"I had to pee," Ivan said, shrugging. "Can you give me my meal ticket?"

The supervisor shook her head sadly. "I thought you weren't coming back. Your trash grabber was snapped in half and all your trash was spilled out. I thought you were pissed with me."

"It was a homeless guy," Ivan said.

"A city truck came and got us shortly after. I tried to look for you."

"Well, what about the confirmation slip?" Ivan asked. "I have to take it to my boss tomorrow."

"Sorry," she said. "They already accounted for us. I didn't give them your name."

"What the hell, lady!"

The supervisor walked away, and the rest of the group followed. "Have a good day, Ivan."

They left him standing at the table, in the space between two songs.

What was he going to do now? Not only could he not eat, but if he went back to work without a confirmation slip, he'd lose his job.

He walked through the festival grounds in a daze. He prepared himself for the conversation with his boss tomorrow. He thought about going back to the office now to get his things.

Ken Gorman worked the late afternoon shift for the city trash workers. He sat at a table, collecting trash grabbers and safety vests.

He'd been a city worker for the last twenty years, and he helped organize the Earth Day events. It was the best achievement in his career so far.

He waited as the guitar player played a new song, the chords echoing across the square. He watched the tremendous crowd of people eating lunch, and the TV crew filming them, and he was content.

A young man walked up to the table with sad eyes.

"Can I help you?" Ken asked.

The young man told him he had been volunteering all day and that his supervisor left his name off the confirmation lists because she didn't like him. He asked if there was any way to get a meal ticket and a confirmation slip so he wouldn't lose his job.

What a sob story. The young man was pretty angry.

Some weird people sure did show up to volunteer at these events.

Ken had volunteered at every Earth Day Trash Fest, and at every one, there was at least one weirdo that he never forgot. This kid looked like the one. He wasn't a weirdo yet, but he was going to turn into one if Ken didn't do something.

"What's your name?" Ken asked.

"Ivan Little."

Ken grabbed a clipboard with a roster on it. He found Ivan's name quickly. The group he was with had already been crossed off. Probably meant this kid was trying to shirk his volunteer responsibilities. Oh, what the hell, he thought, as he crossed Ivan's name off. Then he gave him a yellow wristband and a white confirmation slip. This kid shouldn't have gotten a wristband without more verification, but there were a few left, the event was almost over, and there was no point wasting them. When it came to audit time, it was far better to have run out of food than to have any left. He didn't want to tell the city board that they had allocated too much money for the event. That would be bad news for next year.

"Merry Christmas, kid."

Ivan's eyes lit up, and he shook Ken's hand.

He dashed off into the festival grounds and disappeared behind a portable toilet.

Ken stared after the kid, wondering where he was going. When he realized that he had avoided the weirdo of the year, he smiled and clapped to the music that the guitar guy was playing.

Aside from this exchange, Earth Day was pretty boring this year.

At least he'd gotten a little excitement out of it.

Another group of volunteers approached, and he checked them off his list, giving away the remaining wristbands.

ALMOST DAWN

Rosie Enright stared at her computer screen, blinked several times, cracked her knuckles, ran her hands through her hair, and then declared that she was never going to finish her short story.

Well, finish was an understatement.

She hadn't even started the story.

She had woken up at four in the morning because she'd had a dream.

About a pirate.

And a robot.

On a spaceship.

She had to write this story. Her life as an aspiring writer depended on it.

How hard was writing a short story, anyway?

Only two thousand words, she told herself as she rolled out of bed and put on her robe. Her eyes burned from sleep, but she rubbed them and promised herself that she'd stay awake.

Her bed was only three feet away, and already, after the first sentence, it was calling her back to its warm depths.

Rosie, Rosie, come back to sleep, Rosie...Have some more dreams, will you, Rosie?

She sat at her desk in her pajamas and yawned.

Maybe she needed some tea?

Yes! Tea!

She walked through her dark apartment, afraid to turn the lights on for fear that it would wake up her puppy. If Maisie woke up, there'd be no chance of getting anything done. She'd want to play.

She held her arms out in front of her, feeling the smooth, beveled wainscot that led to her kitchen.

Something stunk in the trash can—probably the shrimp she'd peeled for dinner. She made a mental note to take out the trash later.

She reached into her pantry and beheld her tea selection.

Almost nothing.

The only thing she had was sleepy time tea, and *that* wasn't going to work.

She really needed to visit the organic market more.

Her mother had always told her that she should drink coffee.

But her mom wasn't a writer. Her mom didn't make twenty thousand dollars a year. Besides, coffee just didn't excite her.

She poured herself a cold glass of water from the tap and drank it slowly.

She rubbed her hands together.

"I'm going to finish this once and for all," she said, rolling her neck around.

"The pirate is a handsome guy from the planet Oona," she said, pacing around the kitchen. "Oona has a robot society...no, maybe instead it has a society of blobs. It's a barren, blobby sort of place with a purple sky and green clouds, with oxygen. The blobs don't know anything except how to eat. Thank god for the robots, eh?"

She stopped.

Outside her kitchen window, a black cat balanced itself as it walked across her wooden fence. Its yellow eyes glowed supernaturally as it stared at her for a moment. Then it bounded off into the grass, and she saw its tail disappear into her neighbor's hostas.

She watched the swaying hosta wistfully.

"A cat!" she whispered to herself excitedly. "That's what this story is missing!"

She ran back to her desk and threw herself in front of her computer.

A cat curled up on the deck next to Sid's leg. Sid needed a companion out here in the lonely western quadrant of the Stax galaxy. A cat was better than Jack Daniels...

Oh, Jack Daniels. Jacky Jack. If only she had some.

Her heart sank.

Would they have Jack Daniels west of the Andromeda galaxy? Would alcohol last that long? How would a space colony even make it? Didn't you need wheat, hops, and salt? Where the heavenly heck were you going to get those?

Delete. Delete. Delete.

A cat curled up against Sid's leg.

"That's better," she said.

She stared at her blinking cursor.

He reached down and petted the cat, and the earring in his ear glinted in the moonlight.

Oooooh, an earring...sex-shay!

But why would a narrator say that?

Was Sid the only character?

Was he the viewpoint character?

Would he be able to see his beautiful earring?

Delete. Delete.

He reached down and petted the cat. His earring jangled and he remembered that he needed to clean it.

No, no, no—the last thing she wanted was a dirty pirate.

Delete.

His earlobe hurt. The space where his earring should have been ached, and he brought a hand up to it and could feel that the wound from his duel was healing slowly but surely.

"All right!" she said, pumping her fist. "This is going to be EPIC!"

Her fingers blazed at the keyboard and she wrote so fast that she was surprised when she heard birds singing outside.

The sun rose, sending ribbons of orange and red across the horizon.

Sid slashed the last angry blob and saved the city.

THE END.

Rosie sat back and smiled. Just two hours ago, she had no idea what she was going to do.

She was going to give up.

She was resigned to work her job as a veterinary assistant for the rest of her life.

Nothing wrong with animals, but...

How amazing this was!

She picked a playlist on her phone and played film music. She danced around the room as an orchestra swelled around her, thinking about her story in her mind's eye.

In the shower, she recited the dialogue in the story word for word. As she fed Maisie and walked her, she savored the scenes streaming across her mind's eye.

As she headed to work, she looked at every person in every car on the highway and wondered if they "looked" like someone who could play her characters in the story.

And when she pulled into the clinic, and heard the dogs

barking and running across the backyard, she breathed in deeply. Her muscles ached like she had just finished an intense workout.

She checked herself in the mirror and went to work, all smiles.

Ten years later, Rosie hit the bestseller lists with her novel *The Universal Cadet*. It was about a captain of a space fleet fighting against impossible odds.

She self-published it, and critics loved it.

She sold over twenty thousand copies in the first month alone.

She made enough money to quit her job (the vet assistant didn't thing work out, so she worked for a flower shop).

She paid off her student loans.

She and her boyfriend got married and they had two children.

She lived on the Oregon coast in a big house on the beach.

And she kept writing. And her books kept selling.

One day, she was writing a new novel.

Space opera.

As she sat in her office late one morning, she just couldn't figure out what to write.

Her children were fast asleep and the loud song of crickets and ocean waves blanketed the yard outside.

If she wrote something bad that her readers didn't like, her career would be over. Finished.

She pulled at her hair.

A dear writer friend had told her to write paranormal romances. They were coming back into vogue, and given how hungry readers were, it would be hard to write a bad one.

She had thought about it for a while, but it didn't feel right. It didn't feel fun.

The idea of a space pirate drifted across her mind...

No, too cliché. Waaaaay too cliché.

But wait—didn't she write about a pirate a long time ago?

She struggled to remember, and then it clicked.

Yes! She recalled the story. Sim, or was his name Sid?

She searched through her computer, and then went through her big old filing cabinet that contained everything she'd ever written.

She found it. December 10, 2001: "Sid the Space Pirate."

She shuddered at the name. She must have been trying to be fashionable.

As she read the story, she cringed.

How could drivel like this ever see the light of day? No wonder no magazines had accepted it for publication.

God knows she had sent it out at least one hundred and fifty times. It took two years before she retired it. For those two years, it was her only story. She had written a few other stories but never got around to finishing them. This was her magnum opus at the time.

More like magnum crappus.

Yeeeeck!

But then she remembered how it made her feel. For some strange reason, she remembered that she had written the story at dawn.

Outside her window, it was the bottom of the night, and dawn was fast approaching.

Everything seemed possible for her back then.

If she hadn't written this story, she would have never been a bestseller. Sure, she had written hundreds of things since, but it was her humble beginning.

She set the old manuscript down lovingly on her desk and wheeled back over to her computer.

Her black cat lay curled up next to her keyboard. She stroked him and stared at her computer screen.

Suddenly, she didn't feel so bad.

She started typing. When the first glimmers of sunrise peeked out from behind the clouds, she was already far, far into the wildlands of her next novel.

MAYBE NOW THE STARS WILL SHINE

Agent Devika Sharma crouched in the shadows of a warehouse as a crane hummed to life and swung an arm across the ceiling. She pressed her back against a corrugated wall as a light on the bottom of the crane swept across the floor, narrowly missing her.

In the quick burst of light, she got her first real look at the hostile environment that she'd thrown herself into without thinking.

Shipping containers everywhere, piled two stories high. Latticed rafters with a catwalk high above, a long track of skylights above that. Exactly the kind of breeding ground for criminals she'd expected.

The building shook, and her fingers instinctively twitched toward the handcoil on her belt.

The crane's claws wrapped around an orange shipping container, and a loading bay door opened, exposing the frigid black sky of Cryovox, and a glittering ocean of ice.

A burly man in a parka stood in the doorway, directing the crane.

Devika flipped up the collar on her parka. She rolled across the wide warehouse floor as a bitterly cold gust surged through the building.

She hated the cold. It was the kind that could turn you into a block of ice if exposed too long. She'd heard stories of people dying on Cryovox's surface, stuck standing on the ice, like a giant stalagmite.

She blew on her hands. Her breath rose around her like a cloud of smoke.

She stayed in the shadows as she made her way up a service ladder toward the rafters.

Getting caught would be a very bad idea.

She climbed upward with acrobatic grace, leaping off onto the metal catwalk. Crouching, she got a good look at her targets.

The criminals she had chased halfway across the galaxy.

The two men who were abducting innocent civilians and selling them into the black market.

Her sole mission as a Galactic Police Agent—GALPOL— was to bring them to justice. And give the abducted another chance at life.

And from what she could tell, there was probably a group of people in that shipping container.

God knows she'd spent months tracking them, and she was one bust away from locking up two of the worst specimens humanity had to offer.

As she crawled across the catwalk, she told herself that only the heartless could kidnap men, women and children while on vacation. Pretend to be a taxi ship and whisk them off into space.

That was why agents like her existed—to make them accountable for their actions.

Devika stopped. It was warmer up here, but not by much.

Her bones still had that chilled feeling, like they were covered in frost that she just couldn't shake off.

She spotted two men below. Parkas and stocking caps. About the same height—six feet tall, cream-colored, swarthy skin. Looked like twins.

Both of them had handcoils on their belts. Gray guns with long, needle-like barrels whose bullets could rip through skin like an acupuncturist's worst nightmare.

She'd have to be careful.

She snapped several photos of the men with her phone.

They spoke in hushed tones and gave hand signals to the crane operator, whose back was to Devika.

She photographed the crane, the shipping container, and the skies outside just for a point of reference. Her phone transmitted the images back to the GALPOL headquarters automatically.

She paused, and listened.

"Drop's in two days," one of the men said. He was the less swarthy of the two. "If we get out of here by top of the hour, we'll get there in time."

"Let's go!" the other man said, whistling through his fingers.

The man in the crane swiveled the machine around.

He looked like the other two.

Triplets.

Handsome Guy ran to a control panel and pressed a few buttons.

An entire section of the wall folded, and the warehouse brightened in the cold starry light.

Devika balanced herself in the strong wind. If she hadn't been ready for it, it would have blown her off the catwalk.

She couldn't hear the men anymore.

The wind was too strong.

The duo walked out into the sunlight. Devika spotted a skylight and ran to it, climbing up another ladder, opening the hatch. She eased onto the roof.

The roof was covered in a sheet of ice, and her boots slid on it.

Dropping to her knees, she crawled to the edge of the roof and pulled out a pair of binoculars.

The docks were empty, save for a blue corsair spaceship parked outside the warehouse. A private passenger spacecraft, it looked out of place in this industrial dock, parked on solid ice. Bay doors at the back of the ship were folded out like origami.

Not-So-Handsome Guy waved to the crane with two bright orange marshaling wands.

Crane Guy followed orders and set the orange shipping container on the dock so that the doors were several feet from the corsair bay doors. The container clanged to the ground and cracked the ice gathered on the metal dock.

Handsome and Not-So-Handsome bolted for the container door and unlatched it, straining with all their might to pull the doors open.

Devika drew her handcoil and waited for her opportunity.

Her chance to take them out in two clean shots.

She cocked her shoulder and spoke into a headset on her ear.

"Requesting backup. I've got a visual on three suspects unloading at Dock Seventy-Five. By the looks of it, it's a shipping container full of people. I've got a short window."

Silence.

Then a voice spoke in her ear.

"We hear you, Agent Sharma. Maintain your location and advise."

She lay on her stomach, aiming her handcoil squarely in the space between the container and the ship.

She'd only have a short time to act.

She breathed in, breathed out, felt the air crystallize on her cheeks.

She waited, still as the ice cracking out on the frozen ocean ahead.

Men like these deserved no mercy.

With rotten luck, if there were people in that container, they could all be dead. She'd seen cases where their air supply was cut off, making the shipping container a giant metal coffin.

Another time, she'd seen a container that criminals left behind for one reason or another. The innocents didn't die of oxygen deprivation—they died from starvation.

All that, to be transported across galaxy lines for slave labor. On a moon. Or an asteroid. Where no one would ever see them again, where they'd work like dogs to mine precious metals, then get sent floating off into space with almost no oxygen in their spacesuits when there was no longer a need for them.

And those were the lucky ones.

Handsome emerged from the container with a chain in his hand.

He barked a command, then screamed so that the cords in his neck flexed. He yanked the chain, leading out a dozen naked people and directing them into the ship.

"I've got a visual on a dozen innocents," Devika said. "I'm taking action. Tell backup to hurry."

She sighed, and closed her eyes for a moment.

Something told her to look to her left.

Crane Guy was perched in the driver's seat of the crane, with a sniper rifle. He was scanning the grounds, making his way toward the roof.

Devika instinctively pulled her handcoil over, locked her aim on his head, and fired.

Zzzt! Zzzt!

The needle-like bullets zipped through the air, shattering the crane windows and hitting the man in the head.

CRACK!

The rifle fired, making Handsome and Not-So-Handsome jump.

Devika whipped around and aimed at the shipping container, firing.

A bullet ripped through Handsome's shoulder. He fell into the ship's airlock.

The innocents screamed. Their chains rattled.

Devika fired again.

Zzzzt! Zzzt! Zzzzt!

Not-So-Handsome dashed into the interior of the ship. Handsome grabbed his shoulder and fired at Devika.

She took cover on the lip of the roof, waiting as the shots whizzed by her, so close, she could feel them.

"Get us out of here!" Handsome screamed.

The corsair's engines fired up, a supersonic whirring that filled the area and made Devika want to cover her ears.

She peeked up and fired more shots.

The corsair lifted several feet in the air. The last innocent was barely on the ship. A shivering teenage boy.

Handsome grinned at Devika, then cut the chains that bound the teenage boy.

He grabbed a flare, lit it, and threw it into the icy ocean. An explosion of ice and water made Devika turn away.

When she looked back, the boy was falling through the air.

Arms flailing.

Screams.

Splash.

He hit the water face first. His legs disappeared after him.

Devika's eyes widened.

Handsome fired at her again, but she took cover.

Before she could shoot again, the bay doors closed and the ship swung over the roof, turning in a semi-circle before blasting far over the icy sea.

"Back up!" Devika said.

She waited for a response, but instead heard a screeching, whining metal sound.

She tapped her headset, thinking it was a malfunction.

Then, a tremendous rectangular shadow swept over the roof.

The crane.

In the driver's seat, Crane Guy's body was slumped over the control panel from where he'd been shot.

The arm.

It was falling toward her.

CRASH!

She rolled out of the way just in time as the arm smashed through the ceiling, sending metal shards everywhere.

The arm buckled, swayed, but held.

And then she heard splashing.

The boy.

He was bobbing in the water.

Devika jumped on the crane arm, sliding down it and landing roughly on the ground. On the wall of the warehouse was a life preserver.

She grabbed it and ran to the edge of the dock.

She tossed the preserver.

"Hold on!" she shouted. "Grab it!"

The boy's black hair was stuck to his face and his teeth were chattering. He held on to the life preserver with a shaky grip.

Devika pulled hard. The jagged ice around the hole cracked.

She pulled again, dragging him to the rim. She reached down and pulled him out. They both collapsed on the dock.

She wrapped the blanket around him.

"Conserve your energy," she said. "You've got to warm up."

The boy shivered and brought the blanket around himself.

Devika stood, looking out over the sea.

The duo had gotten away.

She helped the boy into the warehouse, where she set him down against a shipping container.

"My name's Agent Devika Sharma," she said.

"D-Dev...Shar..."

"Take it easy," Devika said, frowning. "What's your name?"

"R-R-ammy. And...T-t-t-t-thank you..."

"You're going to be just fine, Rammy," she said. "I've got police and medics on the way. No one's going to hurt you."

She studied every part of him. He was tall and gangly, like a bad basketball player. Kid probably wore glasses. She wondered what kind of life he lived before being abducted.

She rubbed his shoulders.

"I know you're freezing, but do you have any idea where they're headed?"

He shook his head.

She clucked her tongue and stood, glancing at the dock.

"Me either," she said. "And that worries me."

She studied him again. His shivering was less severe.

"Wait here," she said.

She walked out to the dock as distant sirens filled the air.

She knelt near the shipping container.

The inside smelled strongly of human waste. She wrinkled up her nose.

Those people had been inside for days.

Glancing back at Rammy, she made a mental note to tell him how lucky he was.

She took out her phone and took photos of where the corsair's legs made imprints in the ice. The phone measured the distance between them and produced a small list of makes and models that fit the measurements.

She had been so close.

She had nearly had them.

She replayed the conflict in her mind, thought how she could have handled it differently.

But the truth was that she had handled the situation perfectly. A textbook example of intuition and thinking on one's feet.

And it hadn't been enough.

Her heart broke for those she couldn't save. A knot formed in her throat.

The sirens grew louder, and squad cars swarmed the dock. An ambulance followed behind them.

Devika pointed to the warehouse where Rammy was.

But Rammy wasn't there.

Devika jogged into the building, looking for him.

But the boy was gone.

She called his name, wandering deeper into the warehouse floor.

SLAM!

A door slapped shut and flapped twice.

She saw a foot on the other side, then heard footsteps.

She cursed, then took off after him.

How could someone in such a state run at a time like this?

She burst through the door into a zig-zagging alleyway just in time to see Rammy round the corner.

She ran, pacing herself and her breathing.

She wanted to call his name.

But he wasn't going to stop. That much was clear.

She rounded the corner.

Rammy was up far ahead, running past another warehouse. He slid on a sheet of ice. Devika renewed her energy and dashed after him.

Her lungs were pumping.

Her heart was racing.

Maybe he was scared.

Hadn't she been scared too, when she was eleven years old, running through the jungle forests?

She remembered the grunting, the chainsaws ripping through the trees as her shadowed captors chased her.

The cold, clammy hands of her best friend as he cried in the rain, told her to keep up. And they ran, the mud up to their ankles as lightning struck and thunder shook the forest...

She gained on Rammy, but the road sloped downward and curved around another warehouse, ending on a bridge.

Devika had plenty of chase left.

But the ground was more slippery, and she avoided patches of ice with her peripheral vision. The biting wind nipped at her cheeks.

It was a miracle this kid was still running. Anyone else would have been cowering on the road, turned into an ice block by now.

She exhaled, blading her hands, leaning forward into the slope, letting gravity pull her toward Rammy.

The kid was slowing down.

She was catching up.

Rammy stopped at the end of the road, where a bridge over-looked the frozen sea. The ice was a fifty-foot drop unsur-vivable.

In the distance, a brightly lit city shone under the curve of a transparent dome.

Devika slid to a stop.

Rammy faced the sea, panting.

"Rammy," she said quietly.

The boy didn't turn around.

"Rammy," she said again. "Why are you running?"

She took a step forward.

"You don't have to run. You are safe. The police won't hurt you. We can protect you."

Rammy still did not turn around.

Instead, he climbed up onto the edge of the bridge. He trembled as he stood. He wrapped the blanket around himself.

"I know it's hard," Devika said.

She continued to step forward, hands outstretched.

"Your life has been forever altered," she said. "And that's difficult to accept. But you are strong. You beat them, Rammy. They'll never again touch you."

The wind howled.

"I know there must be so many emotions going through your mind," she said, trying to sound as positive as she could. "I know. One day, not that long ago, I was in your place, Rammy. I was a child slave."

She paused.

"You were?" Rammy asked.

"I wanted to kill myself too," Devika said. "But I got help. And I want to help you. How would you feel if you stepped down from the ledge and we talked about it?"

Rammy didn't answer.

"Rammy," Devika said, trying not to panic.

If this kid jumped, her only eyewitness would be dead. Not to mention any shred of confidence she had about this mission would shatter on the ice along with his skull.

"Rammy, let's talk," Devika said. "Just you and me."

Rammy turned to face her. He was still shivering slightly.

He jumped backward off the bridge.

Devika screamed and reached for him, even though she knew it was futile.

She turned away, bracing herself for the sickening crunch when he hit the ice.

But there was no crunch. Instead, supersonic whirring.

The blue corsair rose in front of her.

Handsome and Not-So-Handsome were in the cockpit, under slanted glass, leering at her. Not-So-Handsome snapped a photograph of her.

The boy sat on top of the glass, relieved the ship had caught him.

And then Devika spotted a black device that he had secretly clipped to his blanket.

A recording device.

She looked back and forth between the boy and the men.

Damn. They were related. Same skin, same hooked nose. Why hadn't she noticed?

A trap.

"We thought it would be a good idea to find out who's been stalking us for the last three months," the boy said. "Thanks for nothing."

Handsome pulled a joystick, and two machine guns extended from the bottom of the corsair.

Devika ran and dove as the corsair fired at her, spraying the bridge with bullets.

She took cover behind a corner, pressing her back against the wall.

"East bridge!" she shouted into her headset.

The squad cars screeched toward her.

The corsair stopped firing and rose into the sky.

The boy climbed into the bay doors and they shut behind him. Then the ship rocketed upward, toward space.

A gray police cruiser ship zoomed over a nearby roof and

gave chase, shooting a stream of bullets after it. The corsair dodged, rolling out of the way.

Devika closed her eyes and massaged her temples.

Fooled.

She had been fooled.

The worst mistake in her career. This wasn't how she wanted to end it!

But she couldn't think about it anymore.

She ran for her spaceship parked two blocks away, hoping she had enough time to catch the bastards.

Devika's sleek black corsair was police-issue. It was an extension of herself. She was glad to climb into the airlock.

She strapped herself in the cockpit, turned the ship on, and wrapped her hand around the control joystick as the ship's engines fired up.

She eased into the sky and prepared the ship for atmospheric exit.

Other police ships blasted off toward the stars, and she followed.

She trained her gaze at the sky.

The ship rattled as she climbed. Even her joystick rumbled. She gripped it hard.

The black sky grew brighter, and in the ship's rearview cameras, the loading docks below grew smaller.

The corsair aimed for an airlock in the dome that surrounded the planet. A large, transparent sliding door opened, and they barreled through it. Behind them, the door closed. Ahead, several miles ahead, another door opened, and they passed through, a straight shot into space. Then their thrusters kicked into full power as they rushed toward the stars.

Devika followed them. The sky darkened and gave way to stars. Devika floated upward, but her seatbelt held her down.

She scanned star-speckled space and steered toward flashing siren lights in the distance.

The blue corsair was flying away from the police ships.

Devika increased her speed.

She flicked a switch and opened her radio, directing a message toward the corsair.

"Stop now," she ordered.

The criminals didn't respond.

A blast struck the wing of the corsair, and the ship slowed down.

And then, more guns extended from the back of the ship.

The police ships unloaded on it, turning the ship into a ball of fire.

Then it exploded.

Devika winced as the flames flashed, then smoldered out. The corsair was a burnt husk floating in the middle of space.

Dead.

The men she was pursuing were dead.

The end of a long chase.

Not the way she wanted it to end.

And those innocent people. God, she didn't want to think about informing the families...

She rested her head against the seat.

More casualties.

Her radio beeped.

"Agent Sharma?"

It was a police cruiser ahead. A male officer.

"Come in," Devika said, closing her eyes.

"Suspects are dead, but you're not going to believe this."

"What?" she asked.

"There weren't any other people on board."

"What?" she asked.

"You had a visual on a dozen trafficking victims. Our scans of the corsair only show three people."

Devika cursed.

"They must have switched the victims to another ship."

Her eyes widened as she realized what that meant.

"Run a list of ships that entered hyperspace within the last twenty minutes."

"Only one," the officer said. "It's long gone too."

Devika cursed again.

"Run faster, Devi!"

The trees blurred by as Devika ran barefoot through the dark forests of Coppice. Thunder shook the ground and the rain fell in great drenching slants, turning the bright jungle planet she had known for the last two years into a darkened, shadow-ridden nightmare.

She panted. Her lungs felt as if they were going to explode.

She wore plastic beads around her wrists, and they shook in frenzied rhythm with her steps.

She didn't know how much faster she could run. She hated the never-ending trees, the shadows, the wetness.

She could hardly see.

"Come on!" a little boy's voice shouted.

And then she spotted a dark hand reaching out for her.

Rajinder—a little boy her age, eleven or twelve. Same age as her. His black hair was matted in a wet clump over his face, and his red cricket jersey was soaked.

He grabbed her hand forcefully.

"We have to keep going!" he cried.

Devika found renewed strength and followed him. His hand was wet and slippery.

They slid down a muddy path. The mud went up to Devi's ankles. Her feet burned from running across soil and rock.

Then the ground sloped upward again. They climbed a small foothill as if it were a mountain. Twice Devika slid backward, but Rajinder grabbed her and pulled her up. They used the trees as support, clawing through the mud until they reached the top of the hill.

Through the broken trees, they spotted a soup of orange lights blinking in the darkness like bokeh from an unfocused camera.

"We're almost there," Rajinder said.

"Do you think he's still following us?" Devika asked, panting.

She looked back. The forest was as dark as the night. The brownish white trees were dull in the rain, like rows of evil teeth.

"Too hard to tell," Rajinder said, hands on his knees. "You going to be okay?"

She leaned on his shoulder to catch her breath. "If it's just a little while longer, I'll—"

A squeal stopped her.

She whimpered as Rajinder grabbed her.

The ground shook, this time from another kind of thunder. Not too far off, several thick trees snapped like twigs.

And then snorting.

Sniffing.

And more squealing. Guttural, gut-wrenching squealing.

Devi fell face-first into the mud. She pulled herself up but slid forward, her back hitting a tree.

The beads on her wrist got stuck on a branch. She tried to

untangle them, but the smooth surface of the beads was covered in mud.

Rajinder helped her up.

"Let the beads go," he said.

She clutched them close to her chest. She couldn't let them go. Not the last traces she had of her mother and father. Without them, she'd have nothing to remember them by.

"No!" she cried. "It's the only thing I have from my parents!"

"You've got your memories," Rajinder said. "It's more than I have of my parents."

"Please, don't take them!"

"Devi, they're making too much noise!" Rajinder said. He ripped the beads off her wrist, and she screamed as they landed in the mud.

She dove for the beads, but before she could grab them, a black boot stomped the ground, covering them.

Boots.

The smell of strong musk, body odor and crusted sweat.

Devi looked up slowly, past the boots, past the potbelly covered in leather and rings, past the chains and shackles hanging from a belt, past the chainsaw gripped by two bulky arms...to a shadowed face with grinning, cracked yellow teeth.

***

Devika woke in a cold sweat.

The bedroom in her spaceship was dark. The stars drifted by, and soft starlight fell on her face.

She checked the clock on her phone. Five o'clock in the evening.

She'd fallen asleep watching the police ships sirening through space and studying the destroyed ship.

She sat up, pushing the sheets aside.

The police would have brought the ship down into the atmosphere of Cryovox by now.

Outside, the icy planet swirled, a reminder of her failure.

She climbed out of bed, stumbled into her bathroom, splashed water on her face.

That memory...

It was the first of the worst, the first of many to come.

How many times had she dreamed it?

How many times would she dream it again before her life's work was done, when all the human trafficking was gone and no children were stolen from their parents and could live without fear?

She balled her fists at the revelation.

In the cracked mirror of the bathroom, she screamed.

Back at the loading docks, she knelt to examine the burnt husk of the ship. The police had dragged it down from space, and it was a miracle it survived re-entry. It was a broken flower of metal, hull curved in on itself with jagged, charred edges.

The frigid landscape cooled it down in a matter of minutes. Frost smoldered on the hull, burning and crackling cold.

The strong smell of smoke hit her as she entered the airlock, looking at where the victims should have been.

She stepped on board, using a flashlight to scan the austere metal walls for hidden hatches.

None.

"Completely destroyed," she whispered, shaking her head.

The ship had gone up in a bloom of flames. Death would have been immediate. No one could have survived an explosion like this.

In the cockpit, paramedics carried out the bodies of the two men and Rammy, covered in white sheets. The stench of roasted death burned her nostrils.

An officer accompanied her. He had a typical, stocky build, and for once, Devika was glad to have some accompaniment on this mission. Still didn't make her feel any better about the situation.

"We found some traces of ice formations on the underside of the hull," he said. "They were fresh."

Devika frowned.

That meant they would have been hiding out in the ice floes around the loading dock. They were waiting to strike Devika, to kill her.

She rubbed her chin. "What's the description of the ship that entered hyperspace?"

"No visuals," the officer said. "And no communications."

It wasn't uncommon for a ship to enter hyperspace with no communications, which was what made tracking illegal activity so difficult. Often, ships entered hyperspace without warning because the operators were experienced, and had no need to radio for assistance. Only ships bearing cargo needed to communicate, get clearance and directions on where to bring their loads.

"Do we have any indication as to the size of the ship?" Devika asked.

"Probably industrial by the signature," the officer said.

"That doesn't make sense," she said.

"Why not?" the officer asked.

Local officers. They didn't understand the ways of traffickers. Almost no one did.

"Traffickers' preferred mode of transport is private passenger ships," Devika said, walking out of the ship.

The loading dock was full of police officers and press.

Photo flashes blinded her momentarily. As her eyes adjusted to the flashes, ghost artifacts sparkled in her peripheral vision, in the ice.

"Unless," she said, "whoever took the innocents didn't leave."

Her eyes widened.

"Maybe they didn't leave," she said again. She turned to the officer. "I need all available units to stop what they're doing and sweep the area."

The officer shook his head. "But—"

"Sweep the area and set up a perimeter outside the planet near orbit, NOW!"

She ran to her corsair, tripping on the ice several times.

***

Devika swerved between two factories, steadying her joystick as she righted the ship and emerged over the sea of ice.

Ice stretched as far as she could see.

Then she swung the ship around, back toward the industrial district, full of falling factories, flat roofs, and cranes.

She increased her altitude, sailing over the roof of a factory. It was empty and abandoned, and she spotted trash through the web of holes in the roof.

Several police ships, blue and white, rose in the distance, crisscrossing each other as they patrolled the area.

She stayed on the lookout for something, anything.

With the district cordoned off, it was just a matter of patience.

Or, futility.

She refused to believe any of this was a waste of time.

She kept scanning the rooftops, flying at a brisk pace.

She steered down to the ice, flying alongside its long, broken windowed façade. She flew inches from the ice.

A metal bridge lay in the distance.

Devika eyeballed the space under the bridge.

Her wings fit.

She maintained her course, increased her speed.

She focused on clearing the bridge.

Out of the corner of her eye, a thruster fired from the underside of the bridge, sending a column of smoke over the ice.

Another corsair—also blue—dashed over the ice, away from the industrial district.

"I've got a visual on a blue corsair heading west," Devika said.

The police cruisers turned in the sky and followed her.

Devika sped up, twirling as she followed the ship back over the rooftops.

She flicked a switch and scanned the interior of the ship. On her dashboard, a wireframe image of the ship appeared. There were thirteen heat signatures inside: one in the cockpit, twelve in the airlock.

"The innocents are on board," Devika said. "The ship may try to escape. Tell the units in space to hold the line!"

Devika activated a machine gun at the bottom of her ship and fired a warning shot. Then she opened her radio and directed a message at the ship.

"You're under arrest. Stop your ship NOW and land, or we will shoot!"

The ship's thrusters blew a renewed rush of flames, and the ship began an upward arc toward the stars.

Devika followed, locking her sights on the ship. It continuously danced out of her crosshairs.

They were nearly to the stars. If she struck the ship now,

and hit—there'd be an engine malfunction, and there'd be no saving the innocents on board. They'd disintegrate in orbit.

The other police cruisers sensed the same outcome, and they held their fire.

Devika prepared for weightlessness, leaning her body into it as she escaped gravity on Cryovox.

She kept the ship in her sights as it hurtled toward the stars.

But the ship cut its engines and slowed.

A line of police cruisers was waiting for it.

There was nowhere to go.

Devika grinned.

"Report to the airlock, get down on your knees, and put your hands on your head..."

Devika stood on a police cruiser as it connected with the airlock of the blue corsair.

She had her hands wrapped around her handcoil, standing in a line with several other police officers.

A firing squad, just in case something went wrong.

Two mechanical saws descended from the ceiling and cut circles in the corsair's bay doors, grinding with a high-pitched whine and throwing sparks into the air.

Devika was never happier or more anxious to see the inside of a ship.

She just hoped that the innocents were alive. All the thermal scanners had reported the criminal in the center of the airlock, unmoving for the last fifteen minutes. A textbook immobilization operation. Nobody who feared for their life ever wanted to piss the police off at this point. Not if they wanted to risk the connection between ships and get blown into space.

The saws finished their cutting, and a new circular, metal doorway fell to the ground.

The air cleared.

Immediately, the police rushed into the doorway, barking orders. Devika followed.

"Hands up! Put your hands up!" they barked.

A lone man in a white tank top was sitting on his knees. The police pushed him to the ground and handcuffed him.

Ranged along the walls were the innocents, hanging naked. Smiles and sighs of relief spread across their faces.

"Everyone's going to be all right," Devika announced. "Everyone's going to be just fine."

Two officers carried the criminal past, and she stopped them.

"Who are you working for?" she asked.

The man, who had a younger, smoother face than she imagined, began to laugh.

"He's going to make sure you burn, Sharma," the man said.

That he knew her name took her off-guard.

"Who?" she asked.

"Who else?" the man asked. "The guy you've been chasing all along, chick."

The police carried him away, leaving Devika standing as if she had been hit by a sledgehammer.

The planet Zachary was different than Cryovox. Where Cryovox was a ball of ice, Zachary was a ball of rock. A pock-marked, scarred landscape of porous rock.

Enemy territory. Enemy to the galaxy. Enemy to humanity.

Neighboring planet, completely different world.

Two warrior ships met Devika the moment she entered

orbit, asked her brusquely what she was doing, and then escorted her down into the planet's dark atmosphere, forcing her to change direction toward a giant crater in the ground.

Devika complied, but wondered if the crater would be her resting place.

As she neared, orange lights in the crater glittered.

A sunken city. It was recessed deep, deep into the rock. Terraced lights angled downward toward a dark infinity.

She landed in the middle of a rocky field.

When she exited, soldiers interrogated her. They wore white armor with glowing neon lines, and helmets with three honey-colored lights at the top—it made them look like insects with coil rifles. She read their body language; they meant to kill her. Keeping an eye on their guns, she flashed her badge. The soldiers relaxed somewhat, but the tension was still there.

They turned and motioned for her to follow.

She walked for a mile under the navy blue sky so full of stars, onto a footpath that wound down into the city.

She got a better look; the city buildings were made from rock, and their exteriors faced outward. People moved in and out of the buildings, making their way ever downward. The smell of cooked meat and spices wafted upward, mingled with exhaust and the smell of other things she couldn't discern. All of the smells merged together into a giant heated column of stink.

As she made her way down the footpath, the smell lessened.

The soldiers opened a door and ushered her through a long, dark hallway with orange lines in the walls that illuminated the path, to a guard post where several soldiers stood on watch. The guards opened the door into a cavern hall. The rock opened up—tall ceilings, stalactites, chandeliers weaved among them, gossamer tapestries in the color of the military—white and orange. The air was damp, water dripped somewhere, and she already had claustrophobia. If this place collapsed, there was no getting out.

"Mr. Miloschenko is occupied," one of the guards said.

Devika pointed to her badge. "I override all appointments. Tell him to get ready."

The guard looked surprised at her retort. He hurried down the hall and opened a door into a sumptuous ballroom carved into the rock. Devika caught a glimpse of men and women in formal wear, dancing in a masquerade. Waitresses carried cocktail drinks around.

Then the soldier shut the door behind him.

Devika waited impatiently.

The door opened again and the soldier motioned to her.

She entered the ballroom. There was a large proscenium stage at the front of the room. A symphony at the foot of the stage changed songs from a bombastic symphony to a slow waltz.

Devika made her way through a crowd of people who looked at her suspiciously.

Zachary people always gave her the creeps. Overtly nationalistic—always talked about how they were an evolution of humanity. They had even formed an empire, hailing an emperor and amassing an army. The government didn't know what to do with them other than to keep them at bay.

She ignored the stares and focused her thoughts on the man she was after.

The lead scientist of the Zachary Empire.

Tavin Miloschenko.

A man who was responsible for the deaths and disappearances of over a hundred thousand men, women and children.

The man who was responsible for the abduction of the twelve innocents she found on Croyovox.

A man without, from what she could tell, remorse.

He had a leathery face, day-old stubble, and graying hair that fell on his shoulders. He wore golden sunglasses and a drab gray suit with a gold chain around his neck.

He was drinking a scotch at a secluded cocktail table, cradling a highball glass in the base of his palm. He raised an eyebrow when she approached.

"Devika Sharma, GALPOL," she said, not wasting any time.

"So?" he asked.

"You mind talking to me in private, or do you want to do this the hard way and talk here in public?"

"A man of my talents," Miloschenko said, "always does things the hard way."

"Fine," she said.

By then, a crowd had stopped to watch.

"All I ask is that you keep your voice down," Miloschenko said. He sat at a white linen cloth table nearby and motioned her to join him.

She grabbed a chair and straddled it backward. The move, deliberate on her part, threw Miloschenko off, and he eyed her suspiciously.

"I know what you've been up to," Devika said.

"Do you mean my successes in weapons technology?" he asked. "Please do tell me about my incredible accomplishments."

"You're trafficking slaves," she said.

Miloschenko laughed. "Why would I do a silly thing like that?"

Devika slid two photographs across the table. One was of the twelve innocents being led off the corsair. The other was of the gruesome corpses of the triplets and Rammy.

"I don't know these people," Miloschenko said, shrugging.

"They know you," Devika said. "And I haven't quite figured out how. But I'm here today to warn you to stop."

Silence.

A new song played, and people began to swirl across the dance floor.

"You're overstaying your GALPOL welcome," Miloschenko said. "You think that because you're galactic police, you can traipse anywhere in the galaxy. But it doesn't mean that you are immune from physical danger, Miss Sharma."

Devika studied his face. His threat was serious.

"Threatening a GALPOL agent is a galactic offense," she said. "Are you sure you want to continue that line of thought?"

"Threatening a leader of the Zachary Empire is foolish," Miloschenko said. "Especially with no proof. The Emperor would be displeased to hear about this." He leaned forward. "But then again, you don't have any evidence to make an arrest, do you?"

She kept her face blank.

He'd called her bluff.

He was smarter than she thought.

"I'm here to give you your one and only warning," Devika said. "We know what you're up to. If you want to do the right thing, release all the people you currently have in your possession around the galaxy. We estimate the current number at about ten thousand. If you do that, maybe we'll drop the investigation. If the human rights violations continue, however, I will personally ensure that you go to jail for the rest of your life and then some."

Miloschenko sipped his scotch.

"Tell me, Miss Sharma," he said. "Of all the things that GALPOL investigates—spacetime crimes, drug smuggling, enemy alien aggression—why do you choose to waste your time on the Zachary Empire? We have been your staunchest allies."

"And violators."

"If you mean the terrible attacks we performed on Traverse II, please know that we were simply asserting our right to defend ourselves."

"By killing innocent people?"

Miloschenko laughed.

"I believe you haven't answered my question," he said.

"GALPOL does not observe special relationships," Devika said. "We observe special crimes, though."

She stood.

"If you see me again, Mr. Miloschenko, it means you're going to jail. And do consider *that* a threat."

Miloschenko stood, flushed.

"And if you see me again... stay on your toes, Miss Sharma," he said.

The comment unnerved her.

Two hands grabbed her.

Security guards.

She pushed them away.

"I can escort myself out," she said.

She walked back to her ship, fully expecting the guards to shoot her in the back.

But they didn't.

As she lifted off and exited the Zachary atmosphere, she told herself that the encounter went better than she thought.

Of course she couldn't make an arrest, but this was the first warning.

Arresting out of the blue didn't seem to work for traffickers.

Especially of Miloschenko's ilk. No doubt she would arrest him when the time came, and she'd lock him away for life.

She looked at herself in the reflection of the cockpit windshield.

This was a never-ending battle. She told herself maybe she should take a vacation. With Miloschenko aware of her now, it was only going to get harder.

But she didn't mind hard.

This kind of hard was easy. Waking up from recurring nightmares?

Harder.

Seeing the faces of children whose lives were ruined just like hers?

Harder.

She punched in coordinates for the GALPOL Headquarters, and told herself this was what it would always be like—running, chasing, outsmarting.

She didn't mind it.

"This isn't over, Miloschenko," she said.

She confirmed her coordinates, tightened her grip around the joystick, and plunged into the bright heart of a nebula.

QUICK—ONLY A FOOL WOULD SAY THAT!

Carter Swanson had an unhealthy attachment to his nine-millimeter.

He had his reasons. A Scrapper crawled into his girlfriend's body while they were making out. He had been kissing Jeanette's warm, wet lips with his eyes closed and didn't see his girlfriend's head balloon into a mushroom-shaped, pustule-covered hunk of grinning teeth dripping with blood and brains until she let out an earsplitting scream that was a mix between a wildcat's and a frightened woman's.

He had to fumble across the room, avoiding katana-sharp claws. He almost died seven times before shooting Jeanette point-blank.

He never left home without his trusty steel ever since.

When a gorgeous woman in a sleek pink dress, red lipstick, and a clipboard insisted that he put his gun in a security screening bin, he stood in a daze as memories of Jeanette came back to him.

The woman smiled with a warmth that made him forget the drab gray room with cracked walls and buzzing fluorescent bulbs for a moment. Her long auburn hair had a shimmering, brown sheen, the kind that reminded him of Jeanette. A silver nameplate on the neckline of her dress said "Hilda" followed by two squiggly red hearts.

Hilda smelled of roses and lavender soap. Nobody smelled like that anymore since the supply chain had been completely destroyed. He wondered who she had to pay to get perfume.

Hilda placed a hand on his shoulder. "Things have changed, Carter. You don't have to worry anymore."

It had been years since anyone had talked to him like that. She spoke in such a familiar tone, like she knew him. Her gentle voice took him back to the before-days, before the Scrappers invaded, before he had to live by the barrel of a gun and the blade of a knife. Before he had to hunt Scrappers down the neon-streaked streets of Gull City. Before you couldn't tell if someone was flesh and blood or had a mushroom-shaped Scrapper in their skull. Before you had to sleep under the stars or in the ass crack of some crumbling bridge and scrounge through dumpsters for half a crust of pizza and ration it into a full day's worth of meals.

Now he had to give up his weapon. He stared at his gun, unable to move. All he had to do was take it out of the holster and place it in the bin. Two seconds. But it now seemed like the hardest thing he'd ever do.

Hilda tilted her head at him and smiled. "Seriously, it's going to be okay. Everyone has to reintegrate back into regular life, you know. This is as wonderful a start as any. I'm going to tag your weapon here and give you this card with a number on it. Kind of like coat checks before the world went to hell, remember? When the event is over, just give this card to me and we'll give you your weapon back."

Carter stared at the coat check card. He had no idea these things still existed.

Hilda winked at him. "But I have a feeling that this pistol isn't your only weapon, is it?"

Carter cursed. The jig was up. He bent down and produced a survival knife from his ankle, pepper spray from inside his pants, a brass knuckle that rested comfortably in a secret pocket in his shirt, and a snub-nosed pistol. Standing there palming his weapons with both hands, he felt naked.

"You really are a true hunter, aren't you?" she asked.

Carter shrugged. "Once a hunter, always a hunter. Even if there aren't many Scrappers to hunt anymore."

The door behind him opened and slapped shut. He jumped and wheeled around. A group of middle-aged women wearing leather walked in, laughing at the top of their lungs. Carter gulped at seeing them. On any other day, in any other building, these women might have been his enemies. They joked among themselves and ignored him.

"Be right with you, ladies," the woman said. She put a hand on her hip and pointed to the screening bin.

"Are you going to participate in tonight's speed dating session or not?" she asked.

Carter took one glance at his gun and then at the group of women.

He put his weapons in the bin.

Hilda led him down the corridor toward a double door with reinforced glass. A metal detector ringed the frame door, its underside glowing in shades of coral and cobalt. "We've got to learn how to live again, you know? Anyway, Carter, we're so glad you're here, and we'll do our best to find you a perfect match."

No one knew for sure what the Scrappers were or where they came from. One report said that they were aliens from a distant planet who arrived on Earth millions of years ago, and the year 2175 was the one they chose to make themselves known. Another report said that they were a mutation grown in a lab in a collaboration between the government and an evil corporation.

But when the Scrappers manifested themselves, the first groups of people to die were astronauts, astronomers, journalists, anyone who worked at a corporation, and all government officials. The Scrappers' true origin was never verified.

They infected the brains of the unsuspecting. The Scrapper would nest inside the human brain, taking control of its host until that convenient time when it went nuclear and completely malformed the host's body into the parasite's true evolution. By then, it had achieved its role in the race's goal of worldwide domination.

This worldwide domination just so happened to bloom on Carter's twenty-first birthday. He was a junior in college and almost finished with a degree in nanotechnology. He had planned to marry Jeanette and start his life.

Instead of graduating with that degree, he graduated with a crash course in survival.

Overnight, the people he knew could no longer be trusted. Overnight, the city began eating itself.

He had to flee his home pod. The only problem was everyone else did too. That he was still alive was a miracle.

When the resistance eradicated the last Scrappers, he didn't believe it. He didn't believe that the old way of life that he had only dreamed about for the last five years was back. And yet here he was at a speed dating event, trying to get back a semblance of normalcy even though Gull City was full of rubble.

As Carter passed through the metal detector and held his hands out to be frisked by a sunglasses-wearing security guard in a dark vest, he couldn't help but laugh.

"What am I doing here?" he asked himself. This whole thing was silly. He had seen a poster and only came because he was curious. He thought about turning back, but Hilda took him by the arm.

She led him into a room so big, it could have been a cafeteria. So many of these buildings had been destroyed in the war that they were barely recognizable anymore. Scorch marks lined the ceiling tiles from a fire long ago. The room had the faint smell of mold and decay. Rectangular, graffitied lunch tables were arranged throughout the room, each with several table tents on them.

Seated at the tables were people dressed just like Carter—in dark, worn clothes that would have helped them keep a low profile in the alleyways of Gull City. Many of them looked around nervously just like him. They didn't belong any more than he did.

Hilda led him to a table where a sour-faced man in a gray hoodie sat pensively. A woman with black curly hair and a leather jacket also sat at the table. She glanced around the room curiously, just as curious as Carter.

"Carter, I'll put you at table B7 if that's okay."

Carter shrugged. "It makes no difference to me," he said.

He didn't see the crack in the floor. Suddenly, he was airborne, his hands stretched in front of him like a superhero. He crashed on the table, pushing it backward. The table struck the woman in the waist and she flew back with a yell.

The next thing Carter knew, he was hugging the table, and she was kissing the floor.

"What's the matter with you?" the woman cried, jumping

up. Her hand instinctively went to her jeans, probably for a knife. But there wasn't one.

Carter jumped back from the table and held out his hands.

"I'm really sorry. Are you all right?"

Hilda ran around the table and helped the woman up. "Miranda, we're so sorry about that."

Miranda settled in at the table, rubbing her head. A tangle of curly black locks fell over her eyes and she tucked them behind her ear. "Talk about seeing stars," she said.

Carter searched Miranda for wounds. She wasn't bleeding. Thank God.

He pointed to the next table. "I'll just see myself over—"

"No, you won't," Hilda said. "The other tables are booked."

"Great," Miranda said sarcastically.

Carter slid onto the bench with a pit in his stomach. He glanced over at the sour-faced guy in the hoodie. The man looked away.

A xylophone glissando played from a speaker somewhere. All eyes turned to the front of the room, where Hilda stood with a microphone. Behind her, two security guards stood at parade rest, staring into nothing.

"Hello, singles," she said. "We are so glad to have you here. This has been a long time coming. I know that love has been the last thing that many of you have thought about these last five years. The Scrappers took away a lot of things. The greatest of those was our relationships."

She began to walk around the room, smiling like a fairy godmother. "But the war is over now. The Scrappers are dead and we have our lives back. The new government has authorized many organizations like mine to begin restoring the old way of life. We are not here to fight each other. We are not here to survive. We are here to do the most fundamental human thing: interact and get to know each other. I just hope that all of you will be able to open your hearts tonight."

Carter resisted the urge to roll his eyes. Miranda did not. She went into a full eye roll. When she saw him stealing a glance at her, she shifted uncomfortably. Carter puffed and focused back on Hilda.

"You will find conversation cards on the table. Please pardon the warm ink. We had these printed just an hour ago with a printing press downtown that was miraculously still operational after all these years. I'm going to set a timer. When the timer goes off, you move clockwise to the next person."

A man at the front table raised his hand. "And... how exactly do we get someone's phone number? The grids are down."

Laughter erupted in the room.

Hilda laughed, herself. "Last I checked, we still have pigeons, don't we?"

With that, Hilda grabbed a concierge bell and tapped a finger on it.

Carter found himself staring at Miranda.

As if awkward couldn't get any more awkward.

Miranda's hair was so curly. She must have found a curling iron because her locks were rolled thick. Many people were finding things in old buildings now that the war was over. She smiled politely at him, exposing a dimple on one cheek.

He wondered what he looked like to her. Hell, it had been years since he looked at himself in the mirror. He wasn't sure if he would like what he saw.

"You're not still seeing stars, are you?" he asked.

"They're mostly gone now," she said.

"Good."

Silence.

Carter picked up the conversation card on the table. As Hilda promised, it was still warm. Printed red letters read, "Describe your favorite memory of Before."

"Just one?" Miranda asked.

"Definitely a tricky question," Carter said. "You want to go, or do you want some time to think about it?"

Miranda glanced up and to the right, thinking.

"I miss ice," Carter said reflexively.

Miranda's face brightened. "I've dreamed about that too."

"A nice cold, tall glass of dark cola," Carter said, almost tasting it on his tongue. "There have been many times when I finished a hunt and wished for something nice and cold."

"You were a hunter too?" Miranda asked.

"Claimed sixteen Scrappers in a day once," he said. "That was my claim to fame...at least before fame died."

"I walked here from Port Timm," she said. "I was a hunter there. Not because I wanted to be."

"None of us wanted to be."

Carter glanced down at the card. "Maybe we'll get lucky and the new government will prioritize ice machines. What's your favorite memory?"

"Lazy Sundays," she said. "Lying on the couch, watching movies with laundry tumbling in my dryer."

"What kind of movies?"

"The cheesy romantic comedies."

"Explains why you're here," he said. "But for the record, I loved those too."

They stared at each other for a moment.

Ding!

"If you could do anything right now, what would it be?" Carter asked, reading the card.

The redhead across from him thought about it for a moment, tapped a finger on her lip, and said, "I have no idea."

Carter shrugged. "So, you've never thought about it?"

"I guess I've been too busy trying to survive."

"Yeah."

No imagination. This one was a keeper.

Not.

Ding.

"What is your ideal date?" Carter asked, reading the next card.

The woman across from him this time was an introspective type. She had short hair and thick glasses. She studied him for a long time, and he wondered what she was thinking.

"I would go do an activity, like rock climbing," Carter said, filling the silence.

The woman looked at him almost in disgust. "Why that?"

"How someone approaches an activity can tell you a lot about them," Carter said.

"I guess you're right."

Across the cafeteria, he stole a glance at Miranda, who was talking to a bearded guy in a brown shirt. She wasn't interested in him, and he wasn't interested in her. Carter looked away before she felt his eyes.

Ding!

"Well, singles, how did it go?" Hilda asked.

No one replied. Hilda's wide smile faded to a slight one.

"All of you are telling me that you couldn't find *anything* to be happy about?"

Silence.

A hand went up. The second woman that Carter had spoken to. The Downer. "It's not exactly easy getting back into the dating scene again, you know."

Carter folded his arms. She wasn't his type, but he had to agree.

"I want all of you to open up to a new experience," Hilda said. "You're still thinking like hunters. The Scrappers are gone. It's okay to let your guards down. Over these last five years, we've all built walls around our hearts. We had to do it to survive, but times are different now."

Her voice took on a pleading tone. "We all must—"

The lights cut off.

A few people gasped. Carter's heart skipped a beat as the generator switched on, and the lights blinked on in a pallid green hue.

"What's going on?" he asked.

A security guard rushed into the room and shut the door behind him. On the other hand, someone fastened a deadbolt.

Carter jumped off the table and to his feet. Everyone else in the room did the same.

The guard whispered to Hilda. Her face went as white as alabaster. For a moment, she struggled to speak.

"It... It...appears we have a problem," she said.

She wrung her hands together. "The guards have just told me that we have an intruder in the building."

Carter pushed his way through the crowd as they erupted into a riot.

"Give us our weapons!"

"Let us out of here!"

Carter instantly regretted giving up his weapons. This room was a barrel, and everyone in it was a fish.

One of the security guards put a hand in front of Hilda and pushed her back. In a gruff tone, he said, "We're sorry, folks, but we can't let anyone out of this room right now."

"And why the hell not?" Carter asked.

Hilda gulped. "Because the intruder is among us," she said. "There is a Scrapper in our midst."

Everyone in the room stood in a giant circle.

Carter's survival instincts flashed back. He stood next to Miranda, who folded her arms and studied everyone in the circle just like he was doing. Now everyone looked suspicious.

Carter stepped into the center of the circle. No one was going to take charge, but someone had to.

"The Scrapper isn't going to come forward, and they're not letting us out of this room, so we're going to have to find it," he said.

"He's right," Miranda said, joining him in the circle. "We have to get creative."

"Anyone got a hacksaw?" the sour-faced man in the gray hoodie asked. "That's creative."

"Yeah, says the guy who's doing the sawing," Carter said.

A woman pointed at the man in the hoodie. "Maybe you're the Scrapper," she said. "That's exactly what a Scrapper would say."

The man shrugged. "Just offering you some solutions. I don't see you offering anything."

Everyone started arguing, and Carter couldn't hear himself think.

"Everyone, stop!" Hilda cried.

Everyone ignored her.

A shrill whistle cut through the room, quieting everyone. Miranda took her fingers out of her mouth and said "Everyone, quiet! Keep talking and you are automatically going to be suspect!"

"Thank you," Hilda said, straightening up. "As I said, this isn't productive—"

"And speed dating *is?*" the man in the gray hoodie asked.

Everyone started arguing again, but Miranda held up a hand and kept the arguing to a light murmur.

Then Carter had an idea.

"That's it," he said. "That's the answer."

"What?" Miranda asked.

"We are here speed dating for love," Carter said. "Maybe we ought to be speed dating for Scrappers."

The room broke into two camps. Carter led the first camp on the left side of the room and Miranda ran the second camp on the right. They divided each camp equally between men and women.

Hilda stood at the front of the room with the bell and a stopwatch.

Ding!

The singles revolved around the graffitied tables.

Ding!

They revolved again. Once Carter was satisfied with the rhythm, he settled into the mix.

Carter studied the Downer woman again. She wasn't so down this time. She looked like someone about to confess a sin. At least, that was what he thought.

"Where'd you come from before you came here?" he asked.

"What's the difference to you? I should ask you the same question."

"Awfully defensive, aren't you?" Carter asked.

The woman shifted. "I went on a jog."

"Like in the Before time?"

"Yeah," she said, lightening. "It helps me take my mind off the stress."

Carter raised an eyebrow. "The stress of what?"

Ding!

"That's exactly what a Scrapper might say."

Carter stared at a heavily tattooed redhead in a vest and camo pants. She was a weather-beaten woman with a dark tan. The After days hadn't been kind to her.

"I find it interesting that you volunteered to be the leader," she said. "Who died and made you the boss?"

"That's a good point," Carter said. "Nobody else took charge, so I did. If I was the Scrapper, do you really think I would want to stand out?"

His logic hit the woman hard. She didn't have a good comeback. "But... But maybe you're using reverse psychology. Maybe that's how you're hiding. In plain sight."

Carter pursed his lips. "Good point."

He didn't have a solid reply to that one.

Ding!

Carter and Miranda divided the room into four camps based on everyone's feedback. Everyone in Carter's group voted on the half they thought were most definitely *not* Scrappers. The other half were the suspects. Anyone who got more than two suspicious votes went into the "suspect" camp.

Miranda followed Carter's lead.

"But how exactly are we going to finish this?" the man in the gray hoodie said, comfortable from the "clear" group on Miranda's side.

Carter stood next to Miranda. "I guess we didn't think that far ahead."

Hilda sat in the corner of the room, hunched up, arms around her knees. She rocked herself back and forth.

Carter sat next to her. She was in the suspect camp.

"That's not making you look any less suspicious," he said gently.

"This was supposed to be a beautiful night," she said. "This wasn't supposed to happen."

"Maybe it's good it did happen," Carter said. "If we're lucky, there will be one less Scrapper in the world after tonight. Their numbers are already low."

Hilda turned to him. "It's not about the stupid Scrappers! Don't you get it?"

The room silenced at her outburst. When Hilda realized all eyes were on her, she stopped speaking and lowered her head.

Carter and Miranda stood on opposite sides of the door, each flanked by a security guard. "We've got the scanners ready," someone said at the other end of the door.

"We need everyone to line up by group in front of the

door," Carter said. "I don't want to do this any more than you do."

"Let's make this quick and easy," Miranda said.

She shared a helpful glance with Carter, and they began corralling everyone into a single-file line.

Despite the original awkwardness, Miranda made for a pretty good partner. She and Carter were on the same page about almost everything.

Maybe everyone in this room was so focused on the old life, unable to give it up. Maybe everyone in this room was incapable of love again. Maybe Hilda was right.

Miranda's "clear" list went first through a rounded metal archway over the door. Carter waited with bated breath as Miranda's line filtered through.

The archway beeped green with each person's passing.

Soon, Miranda's "clear" line was cleared.

"I told you my team was the best," she said, smirking.

Carter pointed to his team and said, "Let's show Miranda and her cronies how good we are," he said.

Miranda folded her arms, swayed a hip, and said, "Yes, let's see."

The last of Carter's "clear" line beeped through.

"See?" Carter said to Miranda. "I'd say we did a great job of clearing the people who were never suspects in the first place."

"You know the drill," he said. He pointed to Miranda's line. "Ladies first."

One by one, the "suspects" filed through the detector.

Beep. Beep. Beep!

All the suspects and Miranda's line were cleared.

Carter cursed under his breath.

"Oh," Miranda said. "Does that make me...the winner?"

"There's a Scrapper among us," Hilda said. "This isn't about winning or losing. Were you listening to anything I said?"

"Sorry, Hilda," Carter said. "I guess this will be over soon."

He wished he wasn't going to lose this competition. He wished that Miranda's group had had the Scrapper.

Someone in his group had been good enough to fool him. He didn't like that. Hadn't he survived all these years? If this had been during the war, he would have died.

He cursed and wished for his nine-millimeter.

"Let's get this over with," he said.

His line filtered through the archway.

Every beep was like a dagger in Carter's heart.

The last person through was the Downer. The archway beeped green over her, and she breathed a sigh of relief. She turned back and gave Carter a slow wave.

"That leaves three of us," Carter said.

Carter. Miranda. Hilda.

"For the record," Miranda said, "I was in the "clear" group. I only stayed behind because that's what leaders do."

"Hilda and I are suspects," Carter said. "Anything final you want to say, Hilda?"

Hilda shook her head.

Miranda skipped through the archway and it beeped green. Miranda pumped a fist and breathed a sigh of relief.

Carter cursed.

Hilda had the Scrapper.

"Well, Hilda," he said, swallowing. "This doesn't look good, does it?"

Hilda smoothed out her pink dress and prepared to make her walk. "You first, Carter," she said.

"No, you're going first," he said, backing away. "But I want to know something."

Hilda hung her head.

"What was the point of all this?" he asked.

"What does it matter if you find love?" she asked.

"It matters if you die," he said. He pointed to the archway. "After you."

Hilda glowered at Carter and glanced between him and the archway. She started to pass through the archway, but just before the scanner beeped, she turned around.

Hilda's head exploded as if it were a Jack-in-the-box full of knives. Carter jumped back and yelled.

Hilda was a parasite dripping with blood in a pink dress. Her head was a demented mushroom. She waddled toward him, breathing with that fetid breath that Carter knew too well. It mixed in with Hilda's rose perfume.

Carter stumbled backward. On the other side of the doorway, Miranda watched in fear as the security guards dropped to their knees and took aim.

He looked for something nearby, but he had nothing. Just his bare hands.

Hilda let out a bone-shaking scream as she leaped for him.

Gunshots erupted from the door. Hilda let out an otherworldly scream and toppled to the floor in a pool of blood. She reached up a mangled hand for him, then it flopped to the floor. Hilda lay curled in a ball.

Carter stared at her in horror.

"Come on through the detector," a guard said calmly, as if the exchange had never happened.

Carter passed through. The archway beeped green.

Miranda found a towel and handed it to Carter. He wiped a smudge of blood from his cheek.

"Pretty sophisticated Scrapper," Miranda said.

"Too sophisticated," he said.

The singles had gathered in the hallway and were decompressing, murmuring about the whole night.

"So much for that," the Downer said, walking out the door. "I knew this was going to be a waste of time."

The others left. Soon, it was just Carter, Miranda, and the security guards, who were cleaning up the mess in the cafeteria.

Carter produced the coat check ticket from his pocket and gave it to one of the guards. The guard disappeared behind a black wall.

"Well, nice to meet you, Miranda," he said. "Too bad this didn't work out. Maybe there's still a chance for us both."

"Maybe," she said.

Carter scratched the back of his head. "I mean, after all, I won. Hilda was technically in your line, remember?"

Miranda threw back her head and gave a full-throated laugh. "We'll have to agree to disagree."

The security guard brought two bins. Carter's with his guns, knives, and pepper spray, and Miranda's with guns, knives, and brass knuckles.

Carter and Miranda spent a full minute in silence rearming themselves before they faced each other.

She extended a hand. Carter took it.

"What do you say we hang out tomorrow?" Carter asked. "Meet me at the crumbling statue park at twilight?"

Miranda smirked. "Just because we survived tonight does *not* mean I'm interested."

"Hard no, then?"

"No," Miranda said, her face hardening.

Carter's heart sank as Miranda drew her pistol and aimed it at his nose.

He put his hands up. "I didn't mean to offend you—"

"Step aside. Scrapper."

Carter sidestepped and Miranda fired two shots.

The security guard behind Carter lay writhing on the floor. Carter jumped back as a rivulet of blood snaked toward his boots.

"I'm losing my edge," he said under his breath.

"I saved you," Miranda said, tucking her gun into her holster. "You can make it up to me."

She walked to the door. The last rays of sunlight streamed through her hair, giving it a golden glow. "Crumbly statue park. Tomorrow at twilight?"

"Hey, that was my idea."

"Was it? I stopped listening when the Scrapper approached from behind and tried to slash your neck off."

"Tomorrow. Deal. Hey, Miranda."

Miranda stopped in the doorway.

"Don't you think it's weird that a Scrapper is the reason we met?" he asked.

"Guess I didn't think about that," she said. "Maybe that means we're doomed, Carter."

She waved and walked into the street.

Carter stood in the middle of the room, eyeing the dead Scrapper, silent security guards mopping up the new mess.

"Love," Carter said, laughing to himself as he pushed out of the building and into the twilight. "Only a fool would say that."

He was so glad to be a fool again.

ONE LAST THING BEFORE WE DOCK

Captain Natalie Fields had just finished delivering a party yacht to deep sea, and she was cruising back to shore when bombs exploded in the distance.

The city was just a sliver on the horizon, but she watched the pier bloom into flames and crumble into the sea, the entire skyline filling with smoke.

Not again.

The wars were on, and this was the third attack in a year.

She was the only one on the bridge tonight. A full moon was rising and it shone brightly through the forward-facing windows. Her instrument panel beeped, and on one its many screens, she watched weather radar drift over the dark screen in shades of green, blue and red. A storm was coming in a few hours, but that was the least of her concerns.

She couldn't get a radio report. The transmission towers were probably taken out in the blasts. The yacht's satellite-based emergency system wasn't picking up any signals.

So the war was really on. And she was the only one on the ship who knew.

Tonight, she had a group of wealthy clients who wanted to see the deep blue sea and drink martinis with dolphins under their feet. The worst kind of tour, really, not the kind of people she wanted to be around. As a premier yacht captain, she had sailed with elite clients—the world's wealthiest, all wanting to get away from the damaged city that seemed to fall apart every time they put it together. Few people could escape like this anymore, and Natalie wondered if even the waters would be locked down someday.

This party wasn't particularly wealthy; one of the women was a model and knew the yacht owner, who cashed in a favor and let them charter the boat at half price.

On land, it was always said that you got what you paid for; it was the same with yacht charters. The party of ten had made an absolute mess of the ship, turning it into a drunken orgy. The crew had to work twice as hard and smile twice as much, so much that Natalie told them to get some sleep early, against the wishes of the party. Given all the crew had been through, Natalie didn't care.

Mallon, the owner, would probably chew her out when she docked.

If he was alive.

But for all the crap he had given her for making her do this run, he just might have saved her life tonight.

She hoped he was okay. He'd given her a chance, and she proved herself on the waters as one of the few black female yacht captains. She'd sailed to six continents and seen more luxury than half the people in the world would ever see in their lifetimes, combined.

Her mind went back to the city. Depending on how bad the blasts were, she realized that she might have been the *only* yacht captain left on the continent.

How was she going to explain this to the crew? That they'd have to reroute to the nearest town and hope for the best?

The crew would understand. They were tough like her.

It was the party that she would have a hard time with.

No, they wouldn't trust a woman who told them that their homes might have been destroyed. They already didn't trust her. Just before they embarked, one woman ("the model") had told one of the crew to clean her glasses when they were perfectly clean. Natalie put the bitch in her place, and it was never the same ever since.

But she wasn't going to tolerate crap on her ship. Not when they should have all been united. It was bad enough on land. It was awkward between them at first, but once the crew started serving food, drinks, and entertainment, then it was okay.

But now all the ugliness would come back double.

They wouldn't believe her about the blasts.

They'd want to go back to the city.

They'd want to see it for themselves.

Natalie calculated the scenarios. If they returned to the city, who knew what would be waiting for them—fire, enemy soldiers, or worse, nothing.

She studied the map; her destination had to be the next city upshore. It was 150 miles north, but probably safe.

She had enough fuel. As captain, she'd always made sure of that. She could always count on the *True Dream* to get her wherever she needed to go. It was a one-hundred-foot motor-sailing yacht. Cruising speed, ten to twelve knots. Enough to make good time on the water and escape pirates. Natalie had enough supplies to last at least two days.

The seas were no place for a woman of color, her father had said.

Yet it was the only place that accepted her for who she was. It was brutally democratic. Lady Ocean didn't care whether you were black, brown or purple; she'd suck you to the bottom of the sea in a storm regardless.

If only others saw it that way.

She checked her watch again and programmed the correct waypoints into the navigation system. She knew these waters as well as her hometown. The boat jumped up and down on the choppy waves, and a chill cut through the air. She pulled her coat tighter and pulled her captain's hat further down over her face.

She had to inform the crew.

She ducked out of the bridge and descended below deck. She walked down an oak-paneled hallway to the crew quarters.

She entered a salon with an oven, small table, and a bathroom. She knocked on two adjoining doors.

After a few moments, they opened.

A sleepy-eyed Latino and a white man with short blonde hair answered, leaning on the door.

"Sorry to bother you," Natalie said.

She never bothered them during their off hours unless there was a problem.

Alan Eulalia, the Latino, wiped his eyes and yawned. He was the chief officer. "What's up, boss?"

Gaston, the chief engineer frowned. "Please don't tell me the party got a second wind."

"The city has been attacked," Natalie said.

"Jesus Christ," Gaston said. "When?"

"Just now. Everything is on fire."

"We have to go back," Alan said.

"No. We are going north."

"Why?" Alan asked. "Forgive me, but—"

"The pier was destroyed. We wouldn't be able to dock even if we wanted."

"And who's to say they haven't bombed their way up the coast?"

Natalie sighed. "I don't know. But all I know is that we can't go home the way we came. I need you to tell the rest of the crew. I'm going to inform the party."

Alan threw on a button-up shirt over his undershirt and he tucked it in haphazardly. "You're gonna need me for this."

Gaston headed to the aft cabin to notify the rest of the crew.

Natalie and Alan continued down the hall toward the living quarters for the party.

"Let's see how they take the news," Alan said, chuckling. "A black woman and a Mexican telling a party full of drunks that their lives are never going to be the same..."

"Not funny, Alan."

Alan yawned again and they passed a porthole, where the waves rushed against the side of the boat.

She wondered what the party was doing.

They were either intoxicated or involved in the biggest orgy of all time below.

She didn't want to know.

Her hands were clammy. She didn't even know if *she* had a home to return to. Or a friend. Or a family. Or a career as a yacht captain. How could she stay strong?

They reached the entertainment room. Natalie knocked.

"Come in," someone said.

They entered a sumptuous movie theater. All ten of the party members were slumped in recliners, watching an action movie.

The room smelled like pot and sweat. Several of the men were shirtless and wore shorts. The women wore sundresses.

"Natalie!" cried one of the men.

A man with blonde hair and a red sweater welcomed her.

He was clearly intoxicated. He shielded his eyes from the sudden burst of moonlight, and he held a can of beer.

"Say, Natalie, would you mind whipping up some hors d'oeuvres? We're starving."

He pointed to a man snoring in a recliner.

She wasn't their slave. She was the captain. She wanted to tell him to go fuck himself, but he was the one paying her bill. Aside from clients like him, the rest of the job was upside.

"I'm sorry, but there will be no more food service tonight, Mr. Danvers. The refrigerators have been restocked and they should have everything you need. But that's not why I'm here."

Everyone quieted.

"You going to ruin our fun again?" Danvers asked. He leaned against a buffet and popped a cashew into his mouth.

Natalie clasped her hands together.

Here goes nothing, she told herself. *Remember, radiate confidence, Captain.*

"The city has been bombed," she said.

"I'm sorry," Danvers said. "Did you say *bombed?*"

"Yes. It is under attack, and we cannot return."

"Like hell we can't," Danvers said. "I'm in the militia reserve. I should be kicking some ass right about now."

"It's too dangerous," Natalie said. "I watched the pier crumble into the water. We cannot dock there. Fortunately, I have come up with a plan, but it's going to require your cooperation, and it's going to require, unfortunately, that you end this wonderful party."

"And if we don't agree?" Danvers asked.

She hardened. She wasn't going to take this much longer.

"I'm the captain of this ship. You don't get to disagree with me."

"My checkbook would disagree."

"In your fee of two hundred thousand dollars for the weekend, you also paid for security. Now, we don't have armed guards on this ship, Mr. Danvers. But you have me. And if you want to forfeit your life and swim back to the city, be my guest. In the meantime, I'm trying to save lives here."

Danvers pursed his lips and held his tongue. He threw the nuts on the floor. "What's your plan?"

"We'll be sailing one hundred and fifty miles north," Natalie said. She paced around the room, trying to read the party.

They were listening. So good so far.

They were scared. To be expected.

"We have enough rations on board to last, but I'll have to ask that all of us, even the crew, conserve and serve smaller portions. I'll also have to travel further out to sea, so the waves may be choppier. I ask that you not use the beach club, for we can't afford someone falling overboard. You may use the sundecks and all the other amenities below deck, but you must remain forward where myself and the crew can see you."

Many in the party nodded their heads and whispered amongst themselves.

"How do we even know that it's safe up north?" a woman asked.

Alan coughed and spoke before Natalie could. "We don't, ma'am. But honestly, we're taking a risk with whatever we do."

That was the best part about having a chief officer. He was always on the same wavelength.

"When we reach the port," Natalie said, "I'll know right away if we're in the clear. If we're not, we'll have to bring the ship into close waters and use the tender to cover the rest of the distance to land. But as long as I'm running this ship, I'll make sure that none of you come to harm."

"What can we do?" the woman asked. She unwrapped her scarf and stood. "If we can help you in any way—"

"You can help by relaxing and enjoying the ship as best as you can," Natalie said. She turned for the door and Alan followed her. "I'll give you updates when I have more information. Thank you."

She exited before they could ask any more questions.

"Nice job," Alan said as they traveled back to the deck.

Natalie stopped.

All this time, she hadn't bothered to look back at the city. She clambered onto a ladder and pulled herself onto the sundeck. She was just below the middle mast, and the sail flapped in the wind.

She leaned over the railing of the ship and pointed to an orange bloom on the horizon. Clouds of smoke billowed into the air.

"My god," Alan said. "It's as bright as a star."

"The good news is we're moving further away from it by the minute," she said.

Gaston climbed onto the other side of the sundeck and waved at them. "We're good," he said. The rest of the crew—two stewardesses, the chef, and the audiovisual engineer—climbed up behind him and waved at Natalie.

She waved back.

They gathered in the middle of the deck and she told them the plan. Then, the rest of the crew scattered to various areas on the yacht, leaving her and Alan standing in the moonlight.

"They're scared, Natalie," Alan said. "The orders are keeping the fear off their minds."

Natalie nodded. The mission at hand was keeping *her* fear away.

They returned to the bridge and Alan took the copilot seat and manipulated the instrument panel.

"At our current speed, we should hit one hundred and fifty miles by sunrise, no problem."

Natalie sank into her seat, staring at the endless waters ahead.

They steered the boat into deeper waters, never taking their eyes off the waves.

The sun rose, making the sea look like rolling fire.

It reminded Natalie of the *True Dream's* maiden voyage, off the Mediterranean coast. The grayish blue water changed in an instant to orange and red, like an Impressionist painting. As she sailed out of port and negotiated her way around small pleasure crafts, the coast fell away and she was free for the first time in her life.

She had sat on the bridge and told herself that this was the greatest job in the world.

It still was.

"We are getting close," Natalie said. "I'll go inform the crew."

"Natalie, two o'clock."

In the orange sea, a boat appeared, about two miles away.

It was a sailing dinghy.

"It's heading for us," Alan said. "Fast."

Natalie thought as fast as she could. Were they coming to attack?

Probably not. This looked like a boat made for pleasure, sailing and fishing. It was long and white.

The chances of them being pirates were moderate, but that didn't make sense either.

She grabbed her radio and spoke into the receiver. "This is Captain Natalie Fields of the *True Dream*. Please identify yourself."

After a moment of silence, a voice came through the radio, but it was in a language she couldn't understand.

"It sounds Russian," she said, turning to Alan. "You speak Russian?"

"Nyet."

"Very funny."

"I don't think anyone in the crew knows Russian, do they?"

"Not enough to communicate properly."

Russians scared her. She didn't understand them and they sometimes had strange ways, especially at sea.

The voice said something again.

"We don't understand you," Natalie said. "Do you speak other languages? Habla español? Vous parlez francais?"

"English," the voice said. "Please stop the ship."

A knot grew in Natalie's throat. Something didn't feel right.

"Stop the ship!"

"That sounds like a threat," Natalie said. "Tell us why you want us to stop."

"Stop the ship!" the voice screamed again. Then it continued in Russian and cut in and out in a staticky wash.

Natalie glanced at the instrument panel. They had enough fuel. They weren't at maximum revolutions per minute yet.

She spoke into the ship intercom. "Attention, everyone. This is the captain. Please retreat below deck. I repeat: please retreat below deck. We will be moving at maximum RPM."

The Russian ship was nearer.

"We're at maximum RPM," Alan said. "We'll never be able to outrun them."

"We're sending a message," Natalie said. "We aren't far from port. If they're going to attack, we'll be close enough to land. Tell the crew to arm themselves."

Alan slid out of the bridge and made his way to aft.

Natalie kept her eyes on the boat, watched as the *True*

Dream passed, and left it behind so that it would have to give chase if it wanted to stop her.

But the boat did not follow.

It kept its course and did not speak to her again.

What was going on?

She watched the radar for a long time before she spoke into the intercom.

"Attention: this is the captain. You may return above deck if you wish. Crew, red alert over."

Alan returned a few minutes later.

"What the hell was that?" he asked.

"No idea."

"I stood on the deck and watched them. They were headed for deep sea."

"I wonder why."

"Who cares now? Let's get to port. That whole exchange made me nervous."

"Five miles away," Natalie said. "I'll notify the crew."

Land appeared, a small strip of brown on the horizon.

The sight of it relieved Natalie, and seeing it, she reduced the RPMs to bring the yacht down to cruising.

No fire.

No bombs.

But smoke. The air was pregnant with it, and they could smell it from the bridge.

The city was not on fire, but it smoked.

As they approached the pier, which was still standing, they saw that there was little of the city left. It was a burnt-out husk, a skyline ready to collapse into dust.

"God," Natalie said.

She had miscalculated. She had used almost all the yacht's fuel. They could not travel much further.

A pit opened at the bottom of her stomach and she wanted to puke.

"What now?" Alan asked. "We're six shades of screwed."

Natalie spoke into the ship's intercom. "This is the captain. We have a problem. We've made it to the next city, but it has been destroyed."

Her voice broke, but she caught herself and paused. "We are almost out of fuel and we have no choice but to dock. The crew and I have arms and we will venture out first. I don't know what we will find, but if we stick together, I am confident we will be fine."

Several cracks sounded from portside, making her jump. Then more cracks.

"That was a gunshot," Natalie said quickly. Her heart raced.

She and Alan made their way across the ship to the port side. The party lay strewn across the tanning deck, and blood was everywhere.

Danvers stood over them and he was panting.

Natalie and Alan held up their hands.

"Drop your weapon," she said.

"There's no home to return to," Danvers said. "I'm not going to let them kill me."

"Who?" Natalie asked.

"The enemy army. I don't care what you think; this is better. At least we can control our fate!"

He still smelled of alcohol. He made no sense.

And if she didn't do something, he was going to kill them both.

Natalie ran at him and punched him in the nose, knocking

the gun out of his hand. She uppercut him and pushed him overboard.

Danvers crashed into the water and cried for help. But the current dragged him under the boat and the propeller tore him to shreds, sending a pool of blood up to the surface.

Alan stared at her, jaws wide open.

"We've got to find the crew," Natalie said. She counted the bodies. All of them were dead.

Gaston and the remaining crew scrambled onto the deck. When they beheld the dead bodies, they put their hands to their mouths.

"Throw the bodies over," Natalie said. "We can't save them."

Alan objected. "But—"

"Alan, I have to worry about the crew now," Natalie said. She had never felt lonelier and more isolated in her life. "Throw them over."

She watched as they threw the bodies into the sea. It was surprisingly easy to watch.

Even if there was a chance of survival, the ship didn't have enough supplies to waste. And there would be no hospitals where they were going.

It was better this way. At least that was what she told herself.

She returned to the bridge and steered to the port.

When she docked the ship and dropped anchor, they gathered on the charred pier and looked up at the remains of the former city.

Perhaps there were survivors in the rubble. She didn't know.

She didn't care.

All she thought about was surviving.

"What do you think we'll find in there?" Gaston asked.

"No idea," Natalie said. She started across the pier. "But we are about to find out."

She didn't hear everyone else's footsteps behind her, but she kept walking.

Then she heard them, slow and measured at first, then frantic as they ran to catch up to her.

It felt weird that she wasn't tackling a problem from the helm of a ship. She preferred solving problems at sea.

But this would have to do.

She looked around at her crew—*her* crew. They looked ahead with conviction and fear.

She knew they were scared.

She was too.

But together they'd be fine.

She smiled and picked up her pace.

Together they journeyed into the city.

ENCORE NO. 1

When you have a superpower, you have to protect it. People without it will take advantage of you. They'll squeeze out your light, chuck you in the trash, and look for the next person to destroy. At least that's what my uncle says.

Me and my uncle have this power of seeing things as they are—and as we want them to be. Take the living room I'm sitting in right now. It may look like a rundown apartment over a pet shop, but if you have my powers, it's actually a sunny French chateau where the house staff serves seven-course meals any time we want them. Open the window, and you can see the crooked skyline of Paris's seventh arrondissement.

Back in 1974, when I was thirteen, my uncle taught me how to use my powers. Me and Mama lived free and nobody bothered us.

But on August 13, 1981, the Scrappers appeared. Mushroom-headed lanky monsters that killed people and assumed their bodies and personalities. Then, out of nowhere, when you'd be kissing your girlfriend—YAOWW!! The thing would split out of her head and chomp you down like a box of Crack-erjacks.

Nobody knows where the Scrappers came from. President Reagan said they came from Russia, just before he started laughing like an insane clown, went Portobello and murdered everybody in the White House. The Russians denied their involvement; they said the Scrappers came from space. But it didn't matter. They were here, and they were taking over the world.

New York City fell first. Then Boston and Philly. Now the Scrappers were in our city and you couldn't trust anybody. Our neighbor next door blew his own brains out in fear. Couldn't take the dread anymore, the thought that even his own family might be Scrappers. You hear stories like this all the time, and also the stories of the people who got chewed up and left in public places as an example of what was waiting for the rest of us.

They got Mama last year. I...don't want to talk about it. The Scrappers murdered her just a few days before my twentieth birthday. I've never been the same. I live with half a heart and an unhealthy attachment to my nine-millimeter. Only way to survive.

I've been living with my Uncle Funky in his apartment ever since.

We've been hiding from the Scrappers. We keep to ourselves when we go out (which isn't much), and when we're home, we live in our little French paradise.

The black side of town is overrun with Scrappers. On rainy nights, you can hear them yowling in the alleys. Their shadows stalk the rain-slicked streets and Lord Almighty help anybody walking home after moonrise. I once saw a Scrapper chew up a woman and her baby just outside our window. Couldn't do a damn thing about it.

But Uncle Funky and I tune all that out as much as we can. One minute, we're listening to someone crying out to God; the next we're breathing clean French air and being waited on by Pierre, our servant who always has a hot meal ready.

But want to know the real secret to our survival?

We can *see* Scrappers. Even when they're disguised as humans. It's kept me and Uncle Funky alive. And nobody has known our secret.

Until now.

"Lenny, it's me. Pick up."

I had just finished dinner. Bouillabaisse with sea bream, potatoes, and mussels. Pierre was cleaning up when the red and gold radio on the table crackled. It was Uncle Funky's magical way of communicating with me.

"What's happenin', Uncle Funky?" I asked.

My uncle's deep hippie voice spoke quickly. He sounded frazzled. Something was up.

"I picked up aloe vera from the grocery store," he said. "It's for that itch I was telling you about. Be there in fifteen minutes. Don't worry about signing for any packages."

My blood ran cold. My fingers twitched toward my nine-millimeter inside my jeans, resting on my hip.

Uncle Funky was always careful how he communicated, just in case anyone happened to eavesdrop. He had just spoken the code words I never hoped I'd hear.

"Aloe vera" meant pay attention. "Itch" meant trouble. "Signing for packages" meant that someone was going to be showing up at our apartment doorstep any minute.

My heart banged like a hammer.

"Keep scratchin'," Uncle Funky said, which meant stay vigilant. "I'm comin' atcha hot." He was on the way.

He disconnected, and the radio went dead.

Pierre bowed. "Be careful, *monsieur*."

I bid him adieu, blinked hard, and I was back in our raggedy apartment. The stale air hit me first, a drastic change from the seafood-laced dinner air at the chateau.

A worn thrift store couch sagged near the curtained windows. The peeling wallpaper sorely needed replaced. The kitchen cabinets needed painting and were separating from the wall in places. Our console television rested on the floor, silent as a sentinel.

I peeked out the curtains and caught a glimpse of my street —sullen brick apartment buildings with windows lit here and there. The roofs were wet from a recent rain, and the moon was high in the starry sky.

A car door slammed like a gunshot and made me duck.

A black government Dodge Diplomat was parked in front of our building. Tinted windows. Two men in black suits and sunglasses stepped out and straightened their ties. One had ruddy cheeks and slicked-back silver hair. His nose was red as if he had just blown it ten times, and he had a pot belly that he shifted his pants to satisfy. He didn't miss any meals, and that was saying something in a world where everyone had to fend for themselves. He was the leader.

The other was a boyish agent who couldn't have been more than thirty years old. Tall and wiry with a face that was as crooked as a Picasso painting.

But that wasn't the only thing I saw. I narrowed my eyes and focused on them. Their skin flashed several times like a beacon, and I saw the human-sized mushrooms hiding inside them, spore-pocked and snarling. The Scrappers perched inside their skulls like venomous spiders ready to strike. Then, the men's skin flashed back to normal.

I cursed under my breath as the men walked into my apartment building.

One by one, footsteps creaked up the wooden steps in the narrow stairwell.

I waited in the shadows, hoped—no, prayed to God that they were coming for someone else. Anyone else in the building but me. Every footstep suspended my heartbeat until I couldn't breathe.

Creak. Creak. Thud. Thud.

Quiet murmurs.

Creak. Creak. Creeeak.

The knock came, flashing my blood to ice water. The raps rang hard and strong, like the knocks before a police raid.

They didn't stop. The men kept knocking for what felt like a minute.

And then I told myself, *Lenny, you dummy, what the hell are you still doing here? You better skedaddle to Seattle, daddy!*

I turned to run when a voice spoke loudly.

—Come on, Lenny— it said. —We know you're in there. Please open the door. We want to talk to you.

That was how the Scrappers got you. Just wanted to talk. No harm in talking, right? Until they scarfed you down.

I lifted open the living room window as soundlessly as I could. A misty night breeze rippled the curtains and blew cold air on my face.

I inched myself onto my windowsill. Our building had a narrow stone ledge that led to a downspout. Uncle Funky taught me how to climb down it in case of an emergency.

Foot after foot, my shoes scraped quietly against the stone ledge as I worked my way toward the downspout, my back against the wall.

The men knocked again, then shouted my name. I could barely breathe.

The cool breeze tickled against my skin as I made progress. Just a few inches now. I reached for the downspout and wiggled my fingers at it. If I could touch it, I could work my magic...

Something yellow above caught my eye.

The sky.

I don't know why, but the pale moon shining in the sky looked so beautiful, so tragic. About a dozen stars winked bright in a semi-crescent under Orion's belt. I had never seen a formation like that before. Somewhere, a horn blared and sizzled into the night as if it were trying to warn me about something. Then, the stars winked again and burned away like dying embers.

I refocused on the downspout.

Wiggle, wiggle...Success!

I caught hold of the downspout and blinked hard, activating my powers. It became an inflatable slide, like the kind they have on airplanes in emergency exits. I jumped on and slid down.

The slide spit me onto the street behind the government sedan. I rolled and ducked behind the car. Seeing the coast clear, I dipped into the alley across the street and ran like Mercury.

I was *flying*, man. If it weren't for the puddles on the ground, you wouldn't have even been able to hear me. The dumpsters in the alley blurred past as I aimed for the golden lights at the end—a bright street where I might be safe for a while.

I only saw a shadow dart from behind a dumpster a half a second before something hit my foot. And then I was *really* flying.

I landed in a puddle. Bounced and rolled. I cried out in pain.

Two men were on me in an instant. Ripped the nine-millimeter from my waist.

—We just wanted to talk to you, Lenny. Why'd you have to go and do that?— one said.

—We must give our thanks to the goddess for blessing our catch tonight— another said.

—Praise be to her who blesses dark alleys and the criminal's sacred stalk.—

Groaning, I looked up. It was the two men in black suits, grinning. Their skin flashed, and the Scrappers in their skulls chomped their jaws and let out a loud YAOWW!!

I fainted.

My eyes opened slowly. A bluish-gray world rippled into focus.

I was in a warehouse. Huge fans whirled in the ceiling. Had to be two stories up.

I was surrounded by shipping containers. I had never seen so many containers in my life. A giant crane hummed and carried a container from one side of the warehouse to another, narrowly missing a catwalk that stretched above overhead. Somewhere, I could have sworn I heard ocean waves. We must have been on the shore somewhere. East side of town.

My hands were tied. To a chair. So were my feet. I struggled to escape, but the ropes were tight.

Quit messin' around, Lenny. Use your powers, daddy!

But—

—Lenny, so glad to have you with us.—

The man in the black suit from earlier. The one with the

ruddy cheeks, red nose, and potbelly. He crouched in front of me and gave me a crooked smile with yellowing teeth.

—We weren't going to hurt you. I don't blame you for fainting. Can we get you some water?—

I scowled at him.

—No water? How about a hamburger? You like hamburgers, don't you?—

"I'd *like* to get outta here," I said finally.

The man in black gave me a crooked half-smile, and then pulled a knife out of his suit pocket. —Yes can do, Lenny.—

I winced and looked away.

—Oh, this? Nothing to be afraid of.—

I winced again as I felt a tug near my arm. I expected the blade to go in any second.

Tug. Cut. Tug. Cut. Tug. Cut.

My arms were free. Then my legs.

—We tied you up to prevent you from hurting yourself.—

The man in black sheathed his knife and put it away. He stood and gestured for me to relax.

—Told you we weren't going to hurt you, Lenny.—

I stood, rubbing my wrists. "What do you want?" I asked.

—We know all about you and your uncle— the man said. — About your *powers*.—

"I don't know what you're talking about," I said as coolly as I could. On the catwalk above, a shadow caught the corner of my eye.

A fringe-tipped suede vest. A lime-green flowery shirt. Dark sideburns and a beard. Uncle Funky crouched on the catwalk. He had a hunting rifle. Seeing me, he put a finger to his lips and disappeared out of nowhere.

—My name is Agent Gibson Cunningham. I'll get down to brass tacks. We need your help.—

Cunningham leaned in close. —What do you see when you see me?—

"A white man," I said.

—That's not all you see, is it?—

"I see you need a dentist."

Cunningham roared in laughter. —Jokes! Come on, Lenny, cut the crap. You know I'm a Scrapper, don't you? You saw my real form the moment I stepped out of my car.—

My eyes widened. I couldn't keep my cool anymore.

—Very good, Lenny. We know what you can do. You can change things, can't you? You can disappear into a world of your own making. This dreary world just fades away and you can forget about us for a little while. Isn't that right?—

I didn't answer him. Above, on the catwalk, Uncle Funky materialized out of thin air. He dropped to one knee and took aim at Cunningham. One shot in the back of the skull, and—

—We need you to show us your powers. We will use it to save your race. We don't want to eat you all the time, but we have to survive, you understand. Our metabolism is quite high. However, we have come to save humanity. We have—

CRACK!

The bullet ripped through Cunningham's skull. The man's body lurched forward.

Uncle Funky fired another shot. Cunningham dropped like a sack of potatoes. Then—

YAOWW!!

The mushroom split from Cunningham's skull with brains dripping from its mouth. It slashed its scythe-like hands and Cunningham's torso cleaved in half. The Scrapper was smeared in blood and guts. Brown gills in its head flapped out like an ancient dinosaur's.

—Fine. You choose to die then, shrimp!—

CRACK!

A bullet tore through the mushroom's body, knocking it down. An instant later, my uncle materialized next to me, grabbed me by the arm, and we vanished and popped two feet away, just before the Scrapper slashed where I would have been.

"Hey now," Uncle Funky said. "That ain't no way to say hello."

He pushed me down and unloaded his rifle into the Scrapper's head. The mushroom shrieked and staggered back.

More YAOWW!!s filled the air around us.

More FBI agents. The Scrappers had split from their bodies and stalked toward us with their foul breath and nasty teeth.

We were surrounded.

—You're screwed, Lenny.— Cunningham said.

"On my lead," Uncle Funky said.

Together we imagined somewhere far from here. The universe pressed on every square inch of my body.

With a POP!, we landed in a park in Paris. The Paris of our imagination. The Paris where there were no Scrappers, no danger, no fear.

It was sunrise. A gaggle of birds escaped from a nearby tree and crisscrossed the sun. A couple strode by with a furry dog on a leash wagging its tail. The cold breeze from the river Seine lazed through the air.

"Phew," I said.

Uncle Funky and I did our secret handshake.

"That was all right," Uncle Funky said. "All right" meant good.

"Thanks, uncle," I said.

"Let's get back to the chateau," he said, taking me by the shoulder. "You cool, Lenny?"

"Better than cool."

We started down the path when a sound froze us both.

YAOWW!!

Behind us was the warehouse we had left. Between it and Paris was a ragged circle of light, a rift between worlds.

Cunningham and the Scrappers had climbed in behind us.

If there's one thing you need to know about my Uncle Funky, it's that he's cool as a cucumber, smooth as silk, Jack. Nothing fazes him. The world could have been ending and he'd barely break a sweat.

Until now.

All the color drained from Uncle Funky's face and he ripped off his sunglasses to see what was really happening.

"How the—"

—Beautiful creation you've got here!— Cunningham said. —You don't mind if we see ourselves around, do you?—

This time, I was the one taking the lead. I grabbed Uncle Funky's hand and we broke into a run.

Cunningham swung behind us, slashing and slashing and gnashing his teeth and calling our names.

We stumbled up some stone steps and into a street. We tore across just before a car blared its horn. The car hit Cunningham and he landed on the windshield. The driver cursed in French and jumped from the car.

We ran down a boulevard with buildings with mansard roofs. Doors and windows passed by in a dizzying blur as Cunningham stayed on our tails.

Scrappers could run forever. We couldn't. But they didn't do well on tricky ground. They were tall and lanky mushrooms.

"I got an idea," I said.

"Shoot."

"Remember that ice planet I created once?"

"How could I forget?"

In an instant, our brains synced and we popped out of Paris. A sky so full of stars wheeled overhead.

Ice skates popped onto our feet and we didn't skip a beat, man. We were speed-skating over an icy planet toward the planet's curved blue horizon. There was nothing around for miles.

It was so cold, it was a wonder we didn't turn into icicles. We were skating so fast, it was keeping us warm.

—Whoooooooawowowo!—

Cunningham slid across the ice like a crazy ballerina, swiping the air. One spore-pocked leg slid up and he smashed his head on the ice.

"Let's leave our man to be a popsicle, you dig?" Uncle Funky said.

"Dig it," I said.

We high-fived and popped back into Paris, on the banks of the river Seine. We were under a bridge. A riverboat eased slowly by, tourists on the decks taking pictures of the famous Parisian riverside. The Eiffel Tower rose solemnly in the distance over the rooftops.

The ice skates disappeared. The rift behind us closed and Cunningham raised his scythes to the air, cursing our names. He was stuck on that ice planet forever. As long as I didn't imagine it again, we wouldn't have to worry about him.

"Good thinking, Lenny," Uncle Funky said. "Let's head back to the chateau."

***

We popped back to the chateau. A series of yowling stopped us dead.

Our chateau was filled with...Scrappers. The floor was covered in brains and blood. The place stunk like diarrhea and rotting fish. The tables were overturned and the windows were broken. The chandelier over the table was shattered into a thousand pieces.

Cunningham stood over Pierre's dead body, waiting for us.

I yelled Pierre's name, but Uncle Funky held me back sadly. Our friend was dead.

—Very unwise, Lenny.—

Uncle Funky materialized a double-barreled shotgun. "Want to dance again, Cunningham?"

"How'd you get in here?" I asked. "This is our world."

—We may be human-eating aliens, but we are superintelligent. We can perceive and interact with your world. Allow me to make my offer again, albeit more forcefully. We want to use your powers to return to our home. You will save humanity in doing so.—

"How are we supposed to trust you?" I asked. I materialized my nine-millimeter and aimed it at Cunningham.

—What do you lose if you do?—

Uncle Funky went "hmph." After a while, he said, "You got a good point there."

—We expected you to be the voice of reason, uncle. Teach your nephew some sense.—

"I got plenty of that," I said.

"We're listening," Uncle Funky said.

—Our ask is simple. We will return to reality. You will open a portal to our home planet. You will keep it open for several hours so that all of our kind may return. Once the last of us have crossed through your portal, you may close it. There is, of course, a catch...—

Uncle Funky and I said nothing.

—You can never use your powers again. We will absorb them completely. It will be an offering to our goddess.—

"Hmph," Uncle Funky said. "And if we don't?"

—We will kill all of humanity. The blood of billions of innocent people will be on your hands now that you know the alternative. We will plaster your faces all over the world and publicize your callousness.—

I don't know how or why, but at that very moment, I heard a woman's voice. She was as loud as if she was standing next to me, but there was no one else in the room. Her voice was pretty.

Lenny, I want you to listen to me. I, uh...know it sounds crazy, but umm, I want to help.

I narrowed my eyes. Was I going crazy?

Gosh, I am so terrible at this. I don't normally talk to my subj—erhm, people. Please, listen to me, Lenny. You and your uncle are in a trap, and no decision you make will get you out. I can. I mean, I will. Will you trust me?

I looked around.

Don't look around. I need you to trust me. I want you to live. You have so much to give, Lenny.

I sure as heck didn't trust the Scrappers. But who was this lady? Why was she talking to me all of a sudden?

As my Uncle Funky would say, I went out on a limb.

Good, you're trusting me. Woo hoo, I'm, killing it! Erhm, okay. Repeat after me.

—Do you accept our offer or not?—

"We'll accept, but under one condition."

Uncle Funky tapped me. "Lenny, what gives, man?"

"Just trust me, uncle. Cunningham, we'll help you, but the portal has to be on a yacht."

—Why a yacht, human?—

"That's our condition. Do you accept?"

Cunningham eyed me suspiciously. He and the other Scrappers gave quick looks at each other. They didn't like it.

Clearly, this woman knew how to rile them. And for that, she was all right with me.

—Very well, Lenny. We will uphold our part of the bargain as long as you uphold yours. But one more thing.—

In an instant, a Scrapper appeared behind Uncle Funky and disarmed him. It grabbed him by the throat and held him high into the air. He sputtered and beat at the Scrapper's scythe-y hand.

—Honor our bargain and your uncle lives. Disobey us and he dies.—

"Lenny," my uncle said. "No matter what happens, I'm proud of you."

I gulped. I sure had to trust this lady now.

It'll all be okay, Lenny. Just stick with the plan.

We left our world and returned to dreary reality where the Scrappers had overrun humanity. Back to the warehouse with all the shipping containers.

The next evening at sundown, when half the sky was twilit and the other half dotted with stars, a mega yacht sailed to the warehouse and dropped anchor at the dock behind the building. It was the biggest yacht I had ever seen, with an American flag flapping on the mast and a full swimming pool on the deck with crystal blue waters. The Scrappers led us onboard and we met the captain—definitely a human—and introduced her to me as Captain Natalie Fields. She was black, with warm eyes and an accommodating spirit. I never met a black yacht captain before. She showed me around the ship and said to ask her if I needed anything. Her generous smile relaxed me despite the tension.

Cunningham tied Uncle Funky to a railing on the deck and

told him that if there was any funny business, he'd be sorry. Uncle Funky and I shared a glance and I told him to be cool.

The lady was still in my ear. At her instructions, I closed my eyes and imagined a portal to another world, a jungle planet with darkened, strange trees with cavernous mouths. A sky dense with ugly white spores. The rotten garbage-y stink of Scrapper drifted from the portal and made me cough in disgust.

The Scrapper's home planet.

—Yes, that is it, Lenny!— Cunningham said excitedly.

At that moment, a semi-circle of winking lights caught the corner of my eye, just over the city skyline. I recognized them from the night Cunningham chased me. The pinpoints of light were bigger than the surrounding stars now.

The lady told me not to look up. I trusted her. Cunningham didn't see the lights. He was too busy drooling at the sight of his mother planet.

I expected Cunningham to jump in. After all, he could've gone home. Instead, another Scrapper jumped out. Then another. And another.

I cursed under my breath. Cunningham lied!

The Scrappers ran to one of the shipping containers and opened it up. The containers were filled with guns.

"You lied!" I cried.

— Thank you, Lenny— Cunningham said as more Scrappers streamed out of the portal. —Close the portal and your uncle dies. Just a little while longer...

I had never seen so many Scrappers in my life. They streamed out of the portal like clowns from a coupe, yowling as they entered Earth.

Meanwhile, the lights in the horizon grew brighter. I couldn't help but look up now. They were as big as comets, and they were traveling fast. Really fast. So fast, that they—

YAOWW!!

The first explosion rocked the warehouse. I fell to my knees.

Something warm and gooey struck me and covered my eyes, followed by the worst stench I've ever smelled in my life. Screams covered the deck.

I wiped my eyes. Those white lights were missiles of pure white, holy light. When the first missile hit, it broke off into lots of little missiles that zoomed around the yacht. Each missile hit a Scrapper and rendered it to goo.

Over the water, white missiles exploded all over the city.

—You betrayed us, Lenny!— Cunningham cried. He ran for Uncle Funky, his scythe hand raised. Uncle Funky didn't stand a chance.

I willed the portal to zip across the deck, in front of Uncle Funky. Cunningham's hand slashed into his home planet instead of Uncle Funky's face.

Uncle Funky grinned, made his handcuffs disappear, and materialized behind Cunningham. When the Scrapper turned around, he met Uncle Funky's fist. My uncle literally knocked Cunningham into a different world. The Scrapper lay on the strange grass, stunned.

"Right on, Lenny!" he cried.

A white missile zipped through Cunningham's chest just as he stood. The Scrapper's black eyes widened as he staggered back. He threw his head into a yowl before he busted apart.

In his place was a woman panting on all fours. Rather, the shape of a woman. She was covered in pulsing black beams of black light that swirled around her like angry snakes. She looked up at me with fiery red eyes and cursed my name. She reached a hand for me, and it lengthened until it almost reached my throat.

The yacht captain pushed me aside and the hand grabbed her instead.

I yelled as the yacht captain's skin and body melted away, revealing the body of another woman, who glowed with white energy. Upon seeing her, the dark woman's hand sizzled away into nothingness.

—Why can't you let me have anything fun, sister?— the dark woman said.

A loud laugh escaped from the pure woman. I recognized her voice as the one inside my head.

"Fun? Oh, this is sooo much fun, sis, but I'm not done yet."

A salvo of white missiles raged into the portal. The Scrapper's home planet erupted in white fire.

—No!— the dark woman cried.

The portal glowed white-hot as the Scrapper's planet disintegrated.

The pure woman turned to me. "Close the portal, Lenny!"

I shut that portal faster than you could say lickety-split. The last thing I saw was the dark woman screaming as her body turned into black rain that splattered across the grass.

The pure woman rose into the air and stretched out her hands. More missiles exploded from her fingertips. Meanwhile, the yacht's horn honked several times, and the boat magically unmoored itself from the dock. Soon, we were setting sail as the bombs exploded along the horizon.

Good thing the yacht was sailing. The warehouse with all the gun-filled shipping containers exploded behind us. The yacht was just outside the radius of the shockwave. A mushroom cloud of pure white energy bloomed over the city rooftops.

Another explosion rocked the warehouse. Uncle Funky grabbed me, and we ducked as my vision filled with white.

Almost all of the Scrappers died that day. The woman's missiles targeted the Scrappers but spared humans.

Turned out she was some kind of goddess. She and her sister dueled across the universe, always taking new forms.

The bad goddess found Earth and decided to infect it with her minions. She sniffed me and Uncle Funky out because she knew we could thwart her plans. She sensed our inner light.

The good goddess told me that humans wouldn't have to worry about Scrappers for a long, long time because Earth was under her control until her sister regained the energy to attack again.

Me and Uncle Funky couldn't believe it as the goddess glowed in our living room and told us that humanity was saved.

You know the craziest part? Nobody knows that me and my uncle saved the world. We prefer to keep it that way.

The goddess blessed me and Uncle Funky with a gift as a thank you. She gave us the ability to see people's inner lights. I could look at someone and know right away if they were compatible with me.

"You've lived in solitude too long," she said. "It's time for you two to find your people."

"That sounds all right," Uncle Funky said, grinning.

Ever since, I've been able to see people's love lights. Some people don't have any, and they are sad cases. Those are the people I know to smile at when I'm walking by, or to go out of my way to do random acts of kindness for. And when I do, I see a little light kindle into existence.

Some people's love lights shine so bright, I can hardly see them.

And some people have that special frequency. I call it the Funky Frequency. You know—they can "see" things like me and uncle. There are more of us than I thought.

Uncle Funky and I are never home anymore. We're always

out volunteering, helping humanity rebuild after the Scrappers. We're always meeting new people. Sometimes we don't come home until midnight because we meet so many new friends. The holiday "Earth Day" took on a brand new meaning, in particular. It became a universal holiday where everyone volunteered to help their fellow humans.

And of course, there are still a few Scrappers left here and there, but when we see them, we expose them for who they are. I dream of the day when that YAOWW!! sound is a memory that new generations never hear.

One night, after volunteering all day for Earth Day, I saw a poster on a telephone pole with a giant pink heart on it.

Speed Dating – Find Love Tonight! Library, 7PM

This was one of the many beautiful ways that humanity was rebuilding itself after the Scrappers.

"Why not?" I asked myself, laughing as I hurried toward the library.

AUTHOR'S NOTES

THE GODDESSES OF CRIME AND JUSTICE

"The Goddess of Crime" and "The Goddess of Justice" were inspired by two distinct events.

The first was a disconcerting dream. I dreamed that I was in a parking garage, walking back to my car. I had this intense feeling of dread, like someone was following me. I kept looking over my shoulder, but there was no one around. Yet, my sixth sense wouldn't stop freaking me out. I felt as if someone was going to pop out from behind a car and harm me.

I never got back to my car because I woke up with my heart pounding.

The next day, I happened to be playing with MidJourney, an AI art generator. I tried to type in a prompt that captured the emotion I was feeling in the dream. The prompt was "League of Villains." It was a black-and white noir image of a group of shadowed, suited villains in a dark city shrouded by shadows. It looked like a black-and-white Edward Hopper painting. I have no idea how I ended up from the dream to this painting, but it happened.

That got me thinking about what type of character could

instill that dread I felt in the dream and also capture the style of the AI art painting.

The idea was a goddess of crime who was an expert in her field. She grew stronger by creating more misery in the world. The story wrote itself. As I was writing it, I remembered, "Wasn't there a Greek goddess of crime?"

Sure enough, there was. This goddess was a (very) minor goddess who almost always appeared with her sister, the goddess of justice. They were the daughters of the more well-known minor goddess of night, Nyx. However, if you look up the two sisters in the pantheon, you'll be lucky if you can find them.

When I finished writing about the goddess of crime, I knew I had to write about her sister, the one in the hospital bed who turned out to be a trickster.

The craziest thing about this story is that I almost finished "The Goddess of Crime" before I remembered that she was an actual Greek goddess. My subconscious must have remembered, though. I even managed to put the goddess of justice in the story *before* I remembered that she was actually real. Really, really eerie how that happens.

When I wrote "The Goddess of Justice," I thought it would be fun to approach the other sister from a different vantage point. The goddess of crime collects her tributes in a city full of crime and misery—in other words, her kind of place. She is in her element and at the height of her powers.

When I wrote her sister's story, I set it in a utopian paradise where justice reigns supreme, where she is at the height of her powers. In this world, the goddess of crime is the oddball out—and now the trickster.

Both stories even have a "Katrina." I'll let you draw your own conclusions on whether it's the same Katrina, but there is a correct answer.

In many respects, you have to read both stories back to back to see the full picture and the push and pull between the sisters and their powers. They are both playing an endless, cyclical game.

Writing both of these stories was a great way to spend a weekend.

HANGIN' WITH UNCLE FUNKY

"Hangin' with Uncle Funky" is perhaps the most autobiographical short story I have written to date.

I was bullied as a kid. All of Lenny's pitfalls with Butch Stokes were really me speaking. I was bullied so much that it was part of my identity growing up.

I also have an uncle who was cool and quirky. When I was a kid, he always gave me advice whenever I had problems, like what to say to a bully, or what to say when I was running for fourth-grade treasurer on my stump speech, or what to write on the note to the girl I had a crush on. He was always there for me, and when I wrote this story, I suppose I was subconsciously channeling my Uncle Terry.

This story is really a story about coming of age and learning how to be comfortable in your own skin. I hope I did that theme justice.

I have also never written a period piece before. The older I get, the more I love and respect the 1970s. It was truly a different time, when our culture was going through turmoil and strife, yet doing it with grace. I had a lot of fun digging through old magazine articles, news clips, and interviews with people in 1974. And, of course, the music...

I am grateful to Kitty Harmon, who read the story from the lens of someone who spent her formative adult years in the 1970s. She helped me get the little details right.

The title of this story came from my proprietary, 100% quirky short story title generator. It's one of my trade secrets that I describe in another author's note in this volume. I learned this technique from Dean Wesley Smith, a prolific writer. The gist of my title generator is that it mashes existing titles from songs, movies, and other media together to create very interesting blends that have a mood of their own. I take the mashed-up creation as a starting point and then modify it to create the title of the story.

Often, my title generator gives me such interesting titles that the stories write themselves. Also, quirky titles are more likely to get readers' (and magazine and anthology editors') attention, so they are also a useful marketing tool. It pays to have good titles.

The first half of the title was inspired by "The Hang-Out" by Dave Grusin. Grusin is one of my favorite jazz and film composers. The song in question is from the *Bonfire of the Vanities* film soundtrack, and its happy-go-lucky mood inspired the restaurant scene in the story. The second half of the title was "Funky the Main Monkey" by Dave Wise from the *Donkey Kong Country 2: Diddy's Kong Quest* soundtrack, possibly one of the greatest Super Nintendo games of all time.

So, in this case, "The Hang Out" and "Funky the Main Monkey" merged together to form "Hangin' with Uncle Funky." As I said, the story wrote itself after that.

I will also mention that "Hangin' with Uncle Funky" was an "almost big time" story. I submitted it to a science fiction & fantasy editor of a major magazine and he loved it. The editor praised the story and bought it on the spot, in less than twenty-four hours of me submitting it. Unfortunately, due to health issues, he had to return the rights to me. The magazine went on an unexpected hiatus. I was sad about that, but I'm glad that I got to include it in the inaugural volume of this series instead. And if you like the Encore story, then you'll know that it wouldn't have been possible without "Hangin' with Uncle Funky." It's just a reminder to me that all things happen for a reason, and everything always turns out for the best in the end.

ALL HALLOWED ROADS & EXODUS RANCH

"All Hallowed Roads" and "Return to Exodus Ranch" take place in my *Last Dragon Lord* dark fantasy universe. *The Last Dragon Lord* is a story about a bloodthirsty dragon lord named Old Dark who seeks revenge against the conspiracy that overthrew him. Dark is one part "Richard III," one part Smaug from *Lord of the Rings*, and one part Francis Underwood from Netflix's *House of Cards*. It's one of my most popular series with readers and one that holds a special place in my heart.

(Dark is the dragon lord referred to in "All Hallowed Roads.")

"All Hallowed Roads" takes place as a side story that happens just before the first major plot point in *Old Dark*. Though "Return to Exodus Ranch" seems to take place in a completely different world, it is in fact the same timeline, just fast-forwarded several hundred years.

Both stories exist independently in *The Last Dragon Lord* universe and have their own standalone power.

I wanted both of these stories to explore the culture and

lore of my elven characters in that series. The elves and dragons in that world don't get along. Elves are prodigious users of magic, and dragons are prodigious hoarders of it. One thing leads to another, and there is a serious power imbalance. And lots of deception from elves, and even more deception from dragons. Anyway, I won't spoil the series because you should read it.

In any case, I wrote these stories after I concluded the trilogy, and it was fun to linger in this world a little longer before moving on to the next series.

If you'd like to explore *The Last Dragon Lord* series, you can do so here: www.michaellaronn.com/thelastdragonlord.

ALONE IN NAKED GREED

This story was inspired while volunteering at an Earth Day event.

I and a group of coworkers signed up to clean up the downtown Des Moines area. We were given trash pokers, trash bags, and wristbands, and our job was to walk up and down a long stretch of grassy road frequented by the homeless and pick up their trash. It was good work, but a little tedious. I found myself craving a hamburger and wondered if anyone would notice if I snuck away down the hill to take a break at a local burger joint. There were hundreds of people picking up trash. But alas, unlike Ivan, I suppressed my hunger.

Several hours later, I found myself a few miles down the road. As the event ended, I turned in my trash and wristband and called my wife, who was supposed to pick me up at the rendezvous point. She wasn't able to for reasons I can't remember. Rideshare services like Uber and Lyft weren't very popular in Des Moines at this time, so I had to walk several miles back to the parking garage where my car was. It was a sunny day with a bright blue sky, striped with fluffy cumulus clouds. As I walked to my car, I conceived this story.

The title of the story was inspired by my title generator. The first part of this story's title, "Alone," comes from a song from the *Saga Frontier* PlayStation video game soundtrack. I don't remember where the "Naked Greed" part came from, but it sounded cool.

ALMOST DAWN

S tories with writers are looked down upon by writers and magazine editors. Some magazines won't even consider a story if the main character is a writer.

This is probably for valid reasons. I can see how many writers would want to write about writers because, well, why not?

I just wrote this story because it was on my heart. I didn't think about how editors would receive it. I sent it out to several magazines, and one editor of a major science fiction and fantasy magazine replied in a condescending tone that stories about writers are pedestrian and not good enough for their magazine.

The response angered me. I had to take a walk around the block. I resisted the urge to reply and tell him I knew a place beneath both of us he could go, but my cooler head prevailed.

And then I realized, this story must have been good enough to get the editor's attention. *I got him to read the story, get worked up about it, and then send me an email with a personalized response.*

How often does that happen? Almost never.

Clearly, I did at least a few things right—if not more.

That was all I needed, and I laughed about the whole exchange before I promptly forgot about it and wrote another story.

MAYBE NOW THE STARS WILL SHINE

This story is set in my *Galaxy Mavericks* space opera series, a multicultural space opera about a group of ordinary people banding together to save the universe.

The heroes of *Galaxy Mavericks* aren't decorated space soldiers; rather, they're everyday people. A soldier from the reserves on his last mission before retirement. An interplanetary real estate agent. A special agent. A garbage man. A cyborg assassin (okay, he's not an everyday person, so humor me). A volunteer with the galactic equivalent of the Peace Corps. Each book serves as their origin story just before they find themselves banding together as a team to fight the villain. Each hero brings a unique skill to the team.

The seventh book is the villain's origin story.

The final two books are typical space opera, planet hopping, swashbuckling, alien battling fare.

This story follows Devika Sharma, whose book is *Zero Magnitude* (Book 3). What's fun about this series is that you can read any of the first six books in any order. So, if you enjoyed Devika's mission, you will love *Zero Magnitude*.

Zero Magnitude begins immediately after "Maybe Now the Stars Will Shine." Tavin Miloschenko's men follow Devika across the galaxy, and they shoot her ship down. She lands on a jungle planet, where she must fight for her life as Zachary soldiers pursue her to finish the job. And that's just the opening scene of *Zero Magnitude*. It only gets crazier from there.

You can learn more about *Galaxy Mavericks* here: www.michaellaronn.com/galaxymavericks.

QUICK—ONLY A FOOL WOULD SAY THAT!

In what could be considered a moment of weakness during a bout of insomnia, I found myself watching speed dating videos on YouTube.

I watched endless videos of couples interviewing each other and trying to find love. Men and women would talk to each other, flirt, ask endless creative questions ("What's your go-to karaoke song?" "Would you rather live in a creepy catacomb or a creepy library?")

You could tell right away if there was chemistry. Just when the conversation would get interesting, the matchmaker would announce that time was up, and the couples would move down the table to interview the next person in hopes of finding their soulmate.

I watched so many of these videos that they ended up on my YouTube recommendation page. When my wife logged in to YouTube on our television, she started asking me some serious questions! I told her it was for research—that classic line that gets writers out of awkward situations every day of the year. (You don't want to know what other things I search for on the Internet in service of writing my novels. One day, if I'm ever investigated by the government, I might have some serious explaining to do.)

Anyway, right around this time, I found myself thinking that I needed to write a science fiction short story. It had been a while, and most of the stories I had written recently were fantasy or contemporary. Somehow, the idea of a bunch of monster hunters speed-dating and trying to get back into romance after a devastating war popped into my head. Right around the same time, I was watching videos of one of the most underrated Sega Saturn video games of all time, *Snatcher*. In that game, humanity lives in a dark cyberpunk future where body-snatching cyborgs pose as humans and kill unsuspecting victims. You often can't tell that someone has been body-snatched. The story follows a detective named Gillian Seed as he investigates the murder of a fellow detective. It's some of the best writing and storytelling of late 1980s video games.

All these inspirations congealed together into "Quick— Only a Fool Would Say That!"

ONE LAST THING BEFORE WE DOCK

I've wanted to write a zombie story, but I've never been much of a zombie writer. Instead, I thought it would be cool to write a post-apocalyptic story.

I was talking to someone who was telling me about their wild adventures working as a crew member on a luxury yacht. Parts of that conversation ended up in this story.

As with many stories I write, I found this story as an opportunity to write a main character I wouldn't normally write about and in a genre that I wouldn't normally write either. I hope the experiment was successful.

ENCORE NO. 1

Wow!

I had a lot more fun with this story than I expected, and I expected to have fun. This is what happens when you take a bunch of stories and collide them together.

A story like this could have been a complete disaster, but I don't think it was. It was actually pretty successful—at least to me.

How do you mash stories together without making it feel like you mashed them together? That was my challenge. Perhaps the story's only failing for me is that you have to have read "Hangin' with Uncle Funky" first. It doesn't quite stand alone, but hey, it's an Encore story.

Easter eggs galore! I'll detail some of them here.

Before we continue, I should caveat that I wrote this story by the seat of my pants. I had no idea what was going to happen until it happened. I don't plan my stories. This keeps me entertained and forces me to keep going so I can know how they end.

The story is a sequel to "Hangin' with Uncle Funky," but set in a separate universe. I never thought I'd return to Lenny and Uncle Funky's world. The original story is still a stand-alone. This story only exists in the world of the Encores and should not be considered an actual sequel.

I took Lenny and put him into the world of "Quick—Only a Fool Would Say That!" purely as an experiment. What would happen?

As I wrote and wasn't sure what to write next, I borrowed from the other stories in this volume as my inspiration. The only stories I didn't borrow from were "All Hallowed Roads" and "Return to Exodus Ranch," and, ironically, "Almost Dawn." I couldn't find a way to integrate them without the story seeming silly.

I chose Lenny as the hero because he had the most to grow. After "Hangin' with Uncle Funky," he's fully awakened to his power. Lenny plays a more active role this time because he's older and more comfortable with his powers. He's using the skills that Uncle Funky taught him.

The Scrappers from "Quick—Only a Fool Would Say That!" were the villains in general and "The Goddess of Crime" is the villain in particular. Lenny admiring the moon and stars and the car horn sizzling away into the night is one Easter egg from the original "The Goddess of Crime" story. So is Lenny getting accosted in the dark alley.

"The Goddess of Justice" appears to Lenny disguised as Captain Natalie Fields from "One Last Thing Before We Dock." The goddess also struggles to speak to Lenny at first, which is an homage to the opening monologue from "The Goddess of Justice."

The Earth Day references at the end are a nod to "Alone in Naked Greed." It could be fun to imagine what "Alone in Naked Greed" would look like if it took place in the world of "Encore No. 1."

The warehouse full of shipping containers is from "Maybe

Now the Stars Will Shine," and so is the ice planet that Lenny and Uncle Funky escape to (mostly).

And the yacht sailing the seas as the bombs explode is a direct nod to the opening to "One Last Thing Before We Dock."

The ending, with Lenny walking to a speed dating event, sets up the story to flow very similar to "Quick—Only a Fool Would Say That!" We can presume that Lenny finds love at the event—along with a rogue Scrapper.

Those are the Easter eggs. There are more.

In a way, this story functions as if all of the timelines from the original stories converged and ran parallel to each other. What a fun experiment.

ADVENTURE AWAITS YOU

If you enjoyed this volume of *Strange Stories*, get ready for even more page-turning short fiction.

Each volume in this series stands alone, so you can enjoy any book in any order.

Visit www.michaellaronn.com/strangestories to explore the full collection!

MEET MICHAEL LA RONN

Science fiction and fantasy on the wild side!

Michael La Ronn is the author of many science fiction and fantasy novels including *The Last Dragon Lord, Android X,* and the *The Good Necromancer* series.

In 2012, a life-threatening illness made him realize that storytelling was his #1 passion. He's devoted his life to writing ever since, making up whatever story makes him fall out of his chair laughing the hardest. Every day.

Connect with Michael
www.michaellaronn.com